THE SHADOW

Entirely unscrupulous and utterly heartless, the blackmailer who calls himself the Shadow is spreading terror across London. The disgruntled servants of prominent members of society provide endless grist for his mill, leading to some of his desperate victims committing suicide. When Sir Richard Bryant, Chief Commissioner of Police, discovers that the mysterious Shadow has infiltrated his own home, even he cannot prevent the murders that ensue; and it is up to Detective-Inspector Carr to track the criminal down before he can escape . . .

DONALD STUART

THE SHADOW

Complete and Unabridged

LINFORD
Leicester

First published in Great Britain

First Linford Edition
published 2016

A catalogue record for this book is available
from the British Library.

119046153

ISBN 978–1–4448–2917–4

Published by
F. A. Thorpe (Publishing)
Anstey, Leicestershire

Set by Words & Graphics Ltd.
Anstey, Leicestershire
Printed and bound in Great Britain by
T. J. International Ltd., Padstow, Cornwall

This book is printed on acid-free paper

Prologue

On a cold night at a time when, looking from Ludgate Circus towards the Strand, the long expanse of Fleet Street was almost deserted, a man came hurriedly from the direction of Wellington Street. He was dressed in a heavy overcoat, with his hands thrust deep in the pockets. He strode along, looking neither to the right nor the left. As he walked, he was gently humming snatches of the latest dance tune that was then being popularised by the radio, and his breath as it left his lips condensed in the frosty air like steam; for the autumn was merging into winter, and snow had fallen on the previous day.

At the entrance to one of those narrow and dingy courts with which Fleet Street abounds, he paused, looked quickly about him, and disappeared within the gloomy opening. Making his way towards a tall block of dilapidated offices, he entered, and began to climb the grimy stone stairs.

He was evidently familiar with his surroundings, for here it was pitch dark, and a stranger would have found difficulty in finding his way.

The late visitor — for it was long past midnight — ascended to the top floor. Before one of the four doors grouped round the landing, he stopped, felt in his pockets for a key, unlocked the door and, crossing the threshold, closed it behind him. His gloved hand felt along the wall and found a switch. Pressing it down, he flooded the small room in which he was standing with light from a single unshaded bulb that hung from the dirty ceiling.

It was not a very prepossessing place. The floor was uncarpeted and, except for a strip of worn linoleum, bare. The furniture consisted of a very old flat-topped table, a chair, and a built-in cupboard. The newcomer locked the door, lit a cigarette, and turned his attention to the wire basket that hung over the letterbox.

Whatever his business was, it apparently demanded a great deal of correspondence, for this receptacle was almost full. Taking another key from his pocket, he unlocked the padlock that secured the letter basket and, taking out the contents, carried them over to the writing table.

Without troubling to remove his coat, he sat down and began rapidly opening the various envelopes. There were all kinds and renditions of letters. Some of the envelopes were cheap, bearing the address in illiterate handwriting. Others, a few, were of an expensive quality. Methodically he slit them all open, placing their contents, unread, in a pile at his elbow. When he had dealt with the last, he swept the collection of empty envelopes to the floor and, taking the first letter from the pile beside him, read it through.

It appeared to be unsatisfactory, for he crumpled it into a ball and tossed it aside. The second followed its predecessor, but the third received more nitration. He read it twice with brows drawn together in a frown, and with a pencil which he took from his pocket, made a brief note near the signature. In this way he went steadily through the entire post, and when he had finished there were only four left for further perusal.

He read these four through once again very carefully, and a smile curved his lips as he did so, for he saw in their contents the possibility of much money. Rising to his feet, he began to collect the empty envelopes along with the other letters he had thrown away. Carrying them over to the small fireplace, he shoved them into the empty grate and, taking a box of matches from his pocket, set them alight.

The mass of paper flared up quickly, and he watched it as it burned. When there was nothing left but a few charred embers, he picked up a short piece of iron that did duty as a poker, and raked about among the ashes until he had reduced them to powder. Returning to the desk, he sat down again, and for a long time remained staring thoughtfully in front of him. The business for the night was completed, but apparently he was in no hurry to go.

Every night for the past month he had

come to this sordid little office at this hour, sorted through the day's letters, kept a few — a special selection, and destroyed the remainder. Sometimes there were more than four worth keeping, sometimes less. He never came in the daytime. During the day the office door remained locked. In any other building this might have led to speculation on the part of the other inmates, but here it passed almost unnoticed. The inhabitants were too busy with their own affairs to bother about other people's. And it is doubtful they even knew that the little door bearing the inscription 'Weekly Gossip' was never opened during ordinary business hours.

The name on the door seemed to indicate that the business carried on behind it was concerned with some sort of newspaper, but if this was the case, the paper was never published; for no order went through from that room to any firm of printers, and the contents of the letters that came daily filling the wire basket behind the letterbox got no further than the brain of the man who read them.

They came from all over the country, from villages and towns, from places scarcely heard of, and from others known throughout the world. A good percentage of them came from London itself, mostly from that small portion popularised by Mr. Michael Arlen which is known as Mayfair.

They were alike in only one particular: they each contained an item of news that was unknown to the general public. Some were written by butlers and ladies' maids, others by footmen and chauffeurs; all came from some class of servant, and each contained something about the writer's employer that was of a scandalous nature. It is a notable fact that only the more lurid of these epistles were kept by the man who received them. The others were of no value to him, for this office had been started with one object only, and that was to put money in the pockets of the man who had rented it. For months he had schemed and planned, and was now reaping the reward for his diligence. Even now, the scheme was only in its embryo state.

The mighty edifice of blackmail which was to rear its ugly head upon that slender foundation was as yet but a figment of his imagination. There was a lot to be done before he could put into practice the idea which his distorted brain had conceived. It was necessary that he should go carefully; one mistake meant disaster, and he was determined that disaster and he should never meet. The ordinary criminal got caught through carelessness, but he was not an ordinary criminal. He had a profound faith in his own intelligence, apart from which, he possessed facilities which the average crook would find it impossible to obtain.

He dropped the stub of his cigarette, ground it beneath his heel, and lighted another. Leaning back in his chair, he gazed up at the cracked ceiling and allowed his thoughts to wander into the future. There was a golden harvest waiting for him if he went to work properly, a fortune that could be had with very little trouble and practically no risk. All that was necessary was care.

Every step must be considered before it

was taken. He had at the outset made up his mind to play a lone hand. There should be no confederate who could give *him* away. All along he had taken the greatest precautions, for this room in which he now sat had been rented by telephone.

The rent for it, a month in advance in lieu of references, he had paid in cash by post. He had never come near the place during the daytime, and therefore nobody had ever seen him. The advertisements which he had inserted, and which had resulted in so many answers, had been typewritten and sent to the various newspapers, together with the amount necessary. In another fortnight he would be able to leave this place for good, and nobody would be able to trace a connection with him. The whole scheme had taken a long time to mature. For over three years he had dreamed and thought about it, overcoming each difficulty as it cropped up in his mind, and now the way was clear to put it into execution.

Already he had settled upon the first three people who were to be made to pay for indiscretions which they, no doubt, considered long since forgotten. He would have liked to be present when they received the letter which he had so painstakingly drafted. The signature, too, was a good touch — the Shadow.

Well, that was exactly what he was: the shadow of their pasts; a shadow that could only be dispersed with money. He hoped the time would soon come when that name would be notorious; when every newspaper would blazon forth an account of his latest exploit. There was a tremendous streak of vanity in his makeup. He wanted the world to become aware of him.

It was for this reason that he had chosen the rather theatrical name with which he had decided to sign his letters. He would get a lot of excitement in reading about himself in print, or discussing himself with his friends and associates. To that would be added the zest of the chase. The police, of course, would leave no stone unturned to run him to earth. He laughed softly. He wasn't in the least afraid that they would ever succeed. From what he knew of them, it would be child's play to elude their clumsy efforts to track him down. Still, it would be amusing.

There was a peculiar kink in this man's brain. Although outwardly there was nothing to show that his mind was unbalanced, as it undoubtedly was, a hair's breadth over the borderline would have led to insanity. He longed for power, and whereas any ordinary person would have chosen to satisfy this longing by achieving fame in business or one of the professions, he definitely preferred a life of crime. The knowledge that he was pitting his brain against the world gave him an enormous sense of satisfaction.

For a long time he sat motionless, smoking cigarette after cigarette, and going over in his mind the details of his plan. It was nearly half past two before he finally rose, brushed the fallen ash from his overcoat, and took a last look round. Unlocking the door, he passed out into the darkness of the landing, and relocked it behind him.

A reporter hurrying homewards from

his tiring day's work saw the man as he turned out of the court, and walked up Fleet Street, and it never crossed his mind that he was looking at a man whom one day the entire police force of England would be seeking. For in that little dingy top room had been born an evil that was to spread throughout the country, leaving in its train misery and death.

1

The Man in the Night

The little closed car nosed its way slowly along the uneven surface of the country lane and presently came to a halt, its long radiator half-buried in the thick hedge that barred further progress.

It was a lonely place, set in the middle of ploughed fields and straggling patches of woodland, where leafless trees reared their tall branches to the dark sky and whispered together eerily as they swayed in the fitful gusts of a cold wind.

The driver of the coupé, a shapeless figure in a heavy leather motor coat, got down from his seat and stood for a moment, peering about him and listening. But save for the faint moaning of the wind and the cracked bell of a far-distant clock chiming the hour, everything was still and silent.

The man who had driven to this

desolate spot at so late an hour counted the strokes — eleven — and as the last note died away he turned from the side of the car and began to walk back along the rough cart track in the direction from whence he had come. The darkness was intense, for the night was cloudy, and he had taken the precaution of switching out his lights, so that the car from two yards away was practically invisible. But this seemed to trouble the man in the leather coat not at all, for he walked with a sure step as though familiar with every inch of the ground he traversed until he came to a gate set in the hedge some two hundred yards up the lane.

It was fastened by means of a chain and padlock, but disdaining these, the stranger pulled himself up, sat astride for a second, and then dropped lightly into the field beyond. A narrow path running diagonally from the gate to the corner of a distant belt of trees cut the field into two irregular triangles, and along this almost indistinguishable track the man set off briskly. It was evident that he had passed this way many times before, for he never hesitated, keeping to the ribbon of pathway with almost uncanny instinct, since it was impossible in that blackness to see the ground ahead. A thin drizzle of rain was falling and, driven by the wind, found its way between the interstices of his coat, causing him to shiver and to thrust his hands deeper into the big pockets as he strode swiftly along.

In a short while he reached his objective — a second gate almost exactly like the first that gave access to a small copse. Climbing this, he turned sharply to his right; and, threading his way among the densely growing trees, presently he arrived at a thick hedge. He walked along by the side of this until he came upon a gap where the hedge had been broken down. Forcing his way through, he sprang across a broad ditch on the other side, and found himself in a narrow road lined by overgrown bushes and tall trees whose gnarled and massive trunks proclaimed their ancient lineage.

The surface of the road was pitted with holes and scarred with deep ruts, and was evidently seldom used except by cattle and farm wagons. The man in the motor coat came to a halt. Glancing about him quickly to assure himself that there was no one else in the immediate vicinity, he took something from his breast pocket and carefully adjusted it about his face. On the other side of the road almost directly opposite the gap in the hedge through which he had come, the vague outline of a building loomed dimly out of the darkness, and towards this the stranger made his way.

It stood a few yards back from the roadway — a tumbledown edifice of rotting, blackened wood that had obviously once been a barn. That it had long been empty and neglected was evident from the crazy condition of the roof, and the fact that the door that should have closed the dark entry lay broken and almost covered with mud on the ground a few feet away.

The thin drizzle had developed into a downpour, coincident with the dropping of the wind, and the man in the motor coat sought the precarious shelter of the ramshackle building with a sigh of relief.

As he entered, he took from his pocket an electric torch, and from the threshold sent its white rays dancing round the interior. If he had expected to find anyone there, he was disappointed, for with the exception of a few rats who scurried away at the unexpected light, the place was deserted. After a hasty glance round, he extinguished the torch, put it back in his pocket and, leaning up against the heavy bulk of timber on which the door had once swung, waited.

The atmosphere of the place was redolent with decay — a peculiar odour of mustiness born of mouldering grain was wafted to his nostrils, intermingled with that curious and indescribable smell which is common to a building that has been long in disuse and become overrun with vermin.

The silence was intense, rendered the more marked in contrast to the patter of the rain on the leaky roof and the splashing of the water that dripped from the broken guttering, which formed an ever-widening puddle in front of the doorway.

The time dragged slowly by, and still the military occupant of the barn remained in the same position — motionless. Evidently he was waiting for somebody, or something, for every now and again he raised his head to listen.

Ten minutes passed — fifteen — and then suddenly to his straining ears there came the sound of a quick footfall crunching on the wet surface of the road. Almost at the same moment, the clock in the distance that had struck before chimed the half hour. The stumbling footsteps drew nearer, paused, stopped altogether, and came on again. Presently a dim figure appeared, a darker smudge against the blackness outside, moving towards the entrance of the barn. As it approached, the man in the motor coat straightened up from his leaning position and spoke.

'You're late, Gelding.' His voice, harsh and metallic, sounded curiously muffled. The newcomer gave a frightened gasp and stopped.

'Gawd!' he exclaimed tremulously. 'You startled me!'

'Why? You expected to find me here,' snapped the other, and then impatiently: 'Don't stand there gaping like a fool. Come inside.'

Gelding accepted the invitation, and advanced hesitantly.

'What made you late?' continued the man in the motor coat. 'I said eleven fifteen.'

'I'm sorry, guv'nor,' muttered Gelding apologetically, shaking the water from his cap. 'I lost me way.'

'Lost your way, how?'

'I took the wrong road at the fork by the station and 'ad to come all the way back,' was the aggrieved reply. 'I didn't find out me mistake until I'd gone close on 'alf a mile.'

The other gave an impatient exclamation. 'I gave you explicit instructions,' he said harshly. 'A child could have followed them.'

'I ain't a child.' Gelding's voice possessed an unpleasant whine. 'Gawd knows what made you choose a place like this.'

'It's good enough for me, and that's

18

sufficient,' retorted the stranger. 'But I don't want to stop here a moment longer than I can help, so let's get to business. What have you got?'

'Letters.' Gelding, who was short and remarkably fat, began to unbutton a voluminous mackintosh.

'Let me see them!'

After a lot of fumbling, the short man produced from an inner pocket a large envelope and held it out. 'There you are,' he said with a note of satisfaction. 'Gems! Every bloomin' one of 'em!'

The man in the leather coat took the packet in his gloved hand without comment and, switching on his torch, walked over to a battered crate which occupied a corner of the barn. Laying the torch down, he opened the envelope and, spreading the contents on the top of the crate, began to examine them. They consisted of six letters, and he read them swiftly, watched eagerly by Gelding, whose red, coarse face, dimly visible in the faint light, was distorted by an unpleasant leer. It was impossible to tell what the other man was thinking, for his face was completely concealed by a mask of black silk that even covered his mouth and chin; but as he finished glancing at the last of the letters and laid it aside, he nodded quickly.

'They seem pretty good,' he remarked.

'Pretty good?' echoed the stout man with a throaty chuckle. 'I should say they was! Masterpieces, every bloomin' one of 'em! What a pity they was written to the wrong man! I wonder what 'er 'usband would say if 'e saw them!' He whistled softly.

'What do you want for them?' asked the masked man shortly.

'Well . . . ' Gelding scratched his head thoughtfully, and his thick lips pursed. 'I was thinkin' about five hundred — '

'Pence or pounds?' snapped the other.

'Pounds, o' course!' was the indignant reply.

'Think again!' retorted the man in the motor coat.

'They're worth it,' protested Gelding. 'Blimey, the lady'd pay more than that for them.'

'Then you'd better take them to her.'

The man in the mask began to gather up the sheets, and Gelding shifted uneasily from one foot to the other.

''Ow much will you spring for 'em?' he asked huskily.

'Two hundred — in cash — now,' was the answer, 'and not a penny more. You can take it, or leave it.'

'It ain't much,' wailed the stout man complainingly. 'I took a lot of trouble to get 'em.'

'Well, that's my offer,' said the man in the leather coat quickly. 'Two hundred, or nothing! So make up your mind, as I haven't got time to waste arguing.'

There was a moment's silence.

'All right,' growled Gelding at length. 'Two 'undred, then.'

'I think you're wise.' The other took a leather wallet from his pocket, and his companion's small red-rimmed eyes glittered greedily as he counted out the notes. 'There you are,' he said. 'Now go! You'll have to hurry if you want to catch the last train back to town.'

'Which way are you going?' enquired Gelding curiously, as he placed the money carefully away in an inside pocket and buttoned up his raincoat.

'That's no concern of yours,' snapped the other, picking up the letters and seeing the cunning look in his companion's eyes. 'Don't you get curious, my friend! Curiosity can kill other things besides cats!'

The stout man shivered at the cold menace in the other's voice, and turned towards the doorway. 'Sorry,' he muttered. 'Good night!'

'Good night!'

The man in the motor coat extinguished the torch, and waited in the dark until his companion's footsteps had receded in the distance and died away to silence. Then he, too, left the barn and, turning in the opposite direction to that taken by Gelding, walked swiftly back through the pouring rain to the place where he had concealed his car.

Two months later, the newspapers rang with the unexpected death of Desiree Gilbert, the well-known musical comedy actress. But there was no one to connect it with that midnight meeting in the lonely barn, or guess that the man who bought those incriminating letters was as surely responsible for her tragic death as if his own hand had administered the fatal dose of the drug that had destroyed her life.

2

The Advent of the Shadow

Sir Richard Bryant, Chief Commissioner of Police for the Metropolis, sat at the big desk in his large, comfortably furnished office overlooking the Thames Embankment; and his stern, rugged face wore a worried expression.

Verging on sixty, he possessed the smooth, clear skin and virile physique of a man of half his years. Indeed, he might easily have passed for forty-five; for his hair, though iron-grey, showed no sign of thinness, and his deep-set slate-coloured eyes still held in their depths the sparkle of youth. For a long time he had sat motionless, ignoring the work that lay waiting at his elbow, and staring with a concentrated gaze at the window. But he saw nothing of the morning sunlight that streamed into the room, or the smoke-grey of the winter sky. His mind was fully occupied with the unpleasant thoughts that had given rise to the troubled frown that wrinkled his usually unruffled brow. During the past eight months it had seldom been absent from his face, for there had appeared on the horizon of crime a fresh personality — a criminal so elusive, so clever in covering up his tracks, that all the efforts of Scotland Yard to check his activities had proved fruitless.

Lady Frayne died from an overdose of veronal, and everybody thought her death was accidental, for apparently this popular society lady had had no worries. It was not until after the inquest that they discovered the letter. It had slipped to the back of a drawer in a little bureau in her bedroom, and for this reason had been overlooked. It was typewritten and contained a demand for ten thousand pounds in exchange for a certain packet of letters, which the writer threatened otherwise to send to her husband. It was signed 'the Shadow'; and when it came into the possession of Lord Frayne, he took it immediately to the police. This was the first inkling they had of the menace which was later to spread a mantle of dread over the whole city.

The Hon. Cecil Glenister, the second son of the Earl of Hoyt, jumped in front of a tube train at Oxford Street Station during one of the busiest hours of the day. Witnesses who had seen the tragedy declared that it was a deliberate action, and that there was no possibility of his having fallen from the platform accidentally. There was no obvious reason why the young man should have committed suicide. He was engaged to one of the most beautiful debutantes of the season, and an investigation into his affairs revealed that he had had no monetary worries.

Somewhere in London, however, a man read of the happening and, opening a little notebook, deliberately crossed off the name of the Hon. Cecil Glenister as being no longer an asset. And the hand that held the pencil was the hand which had typed the letter that had sent Lady Frayne to her death.

Howard Calcott, the eminent K.C., shot himself in his chambers in the temple on the eve of the Mainwaring trial, in which he had been briefed as counsel for the defence. In this case there was no doubt as to the reason of his suicide, for he left behind a letter addressed to the coroner in which he stated briefly that for some months he had been blackmailed by a man calling himself the Shadow, who had in his possession facts regarding an episode in Calcott's life which, if published, would mean his disgrace and ruin. He had paid large sums to this unknown blackmailer, and as a consequence was on the verge of financial disaster. A further sum which he was unable to find had been demanded, and his only alternative was the taking of his own life.

And so the menace of the Shadow spread, until the whisper of his name was sufficient to send a shiver of fear through those whose lives contained a secret they were desirous of keeping from the world. Entirely unscrupulous, utterly heartless, he was that worst type of human parasite, a blackmailer who preyed on the souls of those who got into his clutches, squeezing them dry until bankruptcy or suicide put an end to his persecution.

It had taken some time before the police had become aware of his existence, for naturally his unfortunate victims shrank from seeking aid, fearful that the secret he held over them should become public. Had he ever made a mistake and tried to blackmail an innocent person, it would have been different; but he was apparently much too clever for this, for in no single instance had Scotland Yard received a complaint concerning him. It was only after the deaths of his victims that, as in the case of Lady Frayne, they had received a hint of his existence.

A sudden wave of inexplicable suicides occurred just about this time, and in three cases letters were found among the deceased's effects, bearing the name of the Shadow, and typewritten even to the signature. They were all subjected to the most rigorous examination, and carefully tested for fingerprints, but they afforded not the vestige of a clue to the identity of the sender.

Somewhere, brooding over London like

a spider in its web and waxing fat upon the misery of his fellow creatures, was a man morally guilty of many deaths, but so intangible and wrapped in mystery that no one could give a name or find a living substance for this grim personality who so aptly signed himself the Shadow.

With an effort, the chief commissioner presently roused himself from his reverie and, flicking open a silver box on the desk in front of him, selected a cigarette. Lighting it, he leaned back in his chair with a sigh of weariness. There was cause for his wrinkled brow and general air of depression, for on the previous evening he had had a particularly unpleasant interview with the home secretary, during which that gentleman, who was not given to mincing his words, had pretty strongly hinted that unless Sir Richard could do something to rid society of this pest, and soon, it would be as well if he resigned his position to someone who could.

The latest known victim of the Shadow had been Desiree Gilbert, the popular actress, whose marriage to Lord Aylesbury had been the talk of the London season, and whose tragic death was still the sole topic of conversation among the circle in which she had moved. It was the discovery of one of the familiar Shadow letters among her papers that had precipitated matters, and been the cause of the home secretary's biting remarks that were still rankling in the chief commissioner's mind.

He finished his cigarette, crushed out the stub in an ashtray, and was on the point of turning his attention to the pile of documents and reports that were waiting to be read, when there came a tap on the door, and a uniformed constable entered.

'What is it, Simmons?' Sir Richard raised his head with a frown.

'Miss Lane would like to see you, sir,' replied the man. 'She's in the waiting room.'

The chief commissioner's frown vanished, and he smiled. 'Ask her to come up,' he said, and the constable saluted and withdrew.

The woman who entered a few moments later would have commanded a second glance even in a crowd. Tall and slim, with wide-set eyes that were the colour of a summer sky at dusk, she carried herself with the easy swing of perfect health. Although possessing no truly regular feature, her face was wholly charming and attractive. Sonia Lane in rags would still have been a beautiful woman.

The man who followed closely on her heels was the last person one would have expected to find with such a woman. He might have been any age, but was in reality in his early thirties. A little above medium height, he was weedy, with a pale face and light straw-coloured hair that was brushed straight back from a rather low forehead. His expression resembled that of a particularly unintelligent but amiable sheep; and the weak chin and pendulous lower lip, together with the high eyebrows, caused him to wear a look of eternal surprise, as though he were perpetually wondering why on earth he had ever been born. Most people who were intimately acquainted with Reginald Stimpson wondered the same thing.

Sir Richard rose quickly as they entered and, crossing over to Sonia, kissed her on the forehead. 'My dear, this is rather a surprise,' he said. 'You never told me this morning that you intended to come to town today.'

'I didn't know myself then,' she replied with a smile, 'but when Reggie announced that he was coming, I thought I'd come too, and do some shopping.'

'And I suppose you've dropped in here on the way, to secure the wherewithal?' remarked the chief commissioner with a twinkle in his eye.

'Well, I've only got a pound, Daddy,' she confessed, 'and I want heaps of things.'

'I tried to persuade Sunny to let me lend her the money, old chap,' drawled Reginald Stimpson, screwing a monocle into his right eye and gazing at a corner of the ceiling, 'but she wouldn't hear of it. Bally independent and all that, what?'

Sir Richard took a morocco letter case from his breast pocket and, pulling out three notes, pushed them into Sonia's hand. 'There you are, child,' he said affectionately, patting her shoulder. 'There's fifteen pounds. That ought to see you through.'

She slipped her arms round his neck and gave him a quick little kiss. 'You're a darling!' she said. 'I shan't want nearly as much as that.'

'Well then, you can keep the balance for next time,' chuckled the chief commissioner. He was very proud of this girl who stood smiling before him. Himself childless, he had adopted Sonia when she was little more than a baby and, since the death of his wife two years previously, had lavished all his affection on her, watching her slowly grow to womanhood with pride. It had been a daring experiment from his point of view, for Sonia's father, Simon Lane, had been hanged for the murder of his wife soon after the child's birth. They had both been notorious crooks, and the chief commissioner had watched with anxiety for any hereditary traces to appear in the girl. But they had not, due most probably to the surroundings in which she had been brought up; and by the time she had reached the age of twenty his fears had entirely subsided. He had never had the slightest cause to regret his action in adopting the little orphan, for she could not have given him more love, or behaved more dutifully, if she had in reality been his own daughter.

'Are you very busy this morning?' she asked, putting the money away in her bag and perching herself on the edge of the desk.

'I'm always busy,' said Sir Richard. 'But you needn't go for a moment. Have a cigarette, Reggie?'

'Thanks, old top.' The immaculate Mr. Stimpson leaned over and helped himself from the proffered box.

'What made you suddenly decide to come to town?' asked the chief commissioner as he supplied him with a light.

'Business,' replied Mr. Stimpson. 'Just finished my latest novel, what! You know, the one about the fourteen coffins.'

'Oh, yes, you told me all about it,' said Sir Richard hastily. He knew from experience that if once Stimpson got on the subject of his stories, he would go on for hours. He spent half his life writing completely unpublishable thrillers, and the other half talking about them, firmly convinced that it was merely a matter of prejudice on the part of the publishers that prevented him from becoming a best-selling author.

'Just trotting it along to Lawton and Smith,' continued Stimpson complacently. 'They'll jolly well jump at it.'

'Or on it!' remarked Sonia shortly.

'Oh, really, you know, old thing,' he expostulated, 'that's too bad!'

'I expect that's what they'll say,' she retorted; and then before the exasperated Stimpson could think of a reply: 'You know, you don't look at all well, Daddy.' She eyed him critically. 'Is anything worrying you?'

The chief commissioner's frown returned, and he shrugged his shoulders. 'Nothing more than usual,' he replied.

'By that, I suppose you mean the Shadow?' she said in a low voice.

He nodded. 'I sometimes wonder if we shall ever catch him,' he answered wearily. 'We've done everything that's humanly possible, but he seems to anticipate every move we make, and guard against it. The Home Office are getting very nasty, very nasty indeed. Especially since the affair of this actress woman's suicide.' He paused and rubbed his chin. 'To tell you the truth, my dear, unless something happens soon, I shall have to resign.'

'But it's not your fault,' she protested indignantly. 'You're doing all you can.'

'That doesn't go far with the Home Office people,' he replied a trifle gloomily. 'They judge by results.'

'Do you know, old dear,' Stimpson broke in suddenly, 'I believe I could jolly well help you, what!'

Sir Richard stared at him in amused astonishment. 'You?' he exclaimed. 'What on earth do you know about the Shadow?'

'Oh, nothing, old boy! Absolutely nothing at all.' Reggie polished his monocle vigorously and put it back carefully into his eye. 'But it seems to me that this, er, feller is . . . er, well, different from the other criminal fellers. Out of the common rut as it were, eh!'

'Very much so,' said Sir Richard drily.

'Well,' continued Stimpson, 'I rather flatter myself, you know — '

'It's a habit you've got,' broke in Sonia, surveying a silk-clad ankle.

He looked at her with a slightly pained expression. 'Really, Sunny,' he remonstrated gently, 'you shouldn't interrupt a feller when he's talking seriously.'

'Were you?' she asked demurely, and Sir Richard tactfully turned a chuckle into a cough.

'As I was saying,' went on Stimpson, slightly raising his voice, 'I think I could help you. I flatter myself that I'm rather good at nosing out clues and, er, things of that sort.'

'My dear Reggie,' replied the chief commissioner patiently, 'Scotland Yard is full of very competent men who are good at nosing out clues and things of that sort. It happens to be their job, but they haven't got far with the Shadow.'

'But my dear old lad, that's just where I come in!' explained Reggie eagerly. 'You see, this Shadow feller's rather cute. It wants a peculiar brain to tackle the old joker.'

'You've certainly got that,' declared Sonia emphatically.

'I'm sure it's very kind of you to offer to help,' interposed the chief commissioner quickly, as he saw the expression of hurt annoyance on Stimpson's face, 'but I'm afraid you couldn't do much good. Better stick to your stories.'

'Anyway, old thing,' replied the other, 'I shall jolly well think the matter over. I'm pretty sure that if I spent an hour of close mental concentration on the problem, I should hit on some point that the police have overlooked.'

'I doubt it,' remarked Sir Richard, checking a smile, 'but I shall be interested to hear what conclusions you come to, all the same.'

'In the meantime, we're stopping Daddy getting on with his work,' said Sonia, slipping to the floor. 'You can drop me at Bond Street, Reggie, and then run along to the publishers with your story.'

'Talking of stories,' he began, 'I thought of a simply ripping plot for a thriller this morning. It was cutting myself while shaving that gave me the idea. I'll tell you all about it — '

'Tell me some other time,' said Sir Richard hastily.

'Yes, come on, Reggie.' Sonia walked over to the door. 'Bye-bye, Daddy,' she said, pausing on the threshold. 'I suppose I can't meet you somewhere for lunch?'

Sir Richard shook his head. 'I'm afraid not, child,' he answered. 'I'm terribly busy, and I shall probably have something sent in.'

'All right, then I'll see you at dinner.' She opened the door. 'Coming, Reggie?'

'Yes, old thing.' He extended a limp hand to Sir Richard. 'So long. I'll tell you about that story tonight.'

'You won't!' said Sonia decidedly. 'If you want to tell anyone, you can tell Mrs. Bascombe — if she'll stop talking long enough to listen!'

She laughed, and with Reggie protesting vaguely at her heels, left the office and hurried down the gloomy corridor to the main entrance, where her little two-seater car was waiting.

A tall, good-looking young man who

was just coming in raised his hat at her smile of acknowledgment as she passed him, and stood looking after her from the shadow of the archway until she drove off. Even then he continued to gaze at the receding car, and it was only after it had disappeared among the traffic on the Embankment that he turned and made his way to his office with a sigh.

Sonia Lane occupied a good deal of Detective-Inspector Carr's waking thoughts — more than was good for his peace of mind, as he repeatedly told himself — and it was with a frown that he seated himself at his desk and savagely attacked the work that awaited him; the innocent cause of his annoyance being the immaculate Stimpson, who had helped the lady into her car with an air of proprietorship that was particularly galling to the young inspector's feelings.

3

The Advertisements

His visitors had barely left when the chief commissioner was again interrupted, this time by a thick-set man in a neat suit of blue serge who, after a preliminary tap, stepped briskly into the office, closed the door and approached the desk. Sir Richard, who had looked up rather impatiently, altered his expression as he recognised the newcomer.

'You want to see me, Elliot?' he said quickly. 'What is it, anything fresh?'

Superintendent James Elliot, one of the cleverest of the 'Big Four,' drew forward a chair and, without waiting for his superior's permission, sat down. 'I think I've got a line to the Shadow, sir,' he said briefly.

The grey-haired man leaned forward, his eyes gleaming. 'How did you manage it?' he asked eagerly.

'For a long time I've been trying to discover the method by which he gets his information,' replied Elliot. 'It's always puzzled me how he managed that, and now — I think I know.' He took an envelope from his pocket. 'I'm not absolutely certain yet,' he continued, 'but I shall be by this time tomorrow.' He opened the envelope and withdrew several newspaper cuttings, which he pushed across the desk towards the commissioner. 'During the past eighteen months, these have been appearing at irregular intervals. As you will see, the wording in nearly every case is the same.'

Sir Richard picked up the slips one by one and read them with a frown. The first ran:

'A. B. — Letters waiting. Will forward if send address. W.'

The second was worded exactly the same, except for the final letter, which was a D. The third was slightly different:

'A. B. — Documents ready. Awaiting

instructions. L. M.'

'They appeared in the personal columns on various occasions,' said the superintendent, 'and it's my opinion that it is in this way that the people who have information to sell communicate the fact to the Shadow.'

'What makes you think that?' asked the chief commissioner.

Elliot cleared his throat and hitched his chair a little closer to the desk. 'Lady Frayne had a French maid whom she discharged for theft, sir,' he said. 'The girl has left the country, but her name was Doumant — Marie Doumant.'

He paused, and Sir Richard looked at him a little blankly. 'I'm afraid I don't quite see the connection,' said the latter.

'The signature letter in one of those advertisements is a D,' explained the superintendent, leaning over and pointing it out. 'The Hon. Cecil Glenister had his pocket picked six months before he committed suicide, and the man who did it was a little dip named Wylie. We pulled him in afterwards on another charge, and

43

he admitted it. Howard Calcott had a clerk called Leslie Mason whom he discharged for incompetence. Now, sir, do you see what I mean?'

The commissioner drew a long breath. 'Yes,' he said, 'and I must say that I think you've done an extraordinarily clever piece of work, Elliot.'

The superintendent's face showed his gratification. 'I may be entirely wrong, sir,' he said, 'but still I think it's worth following up. You see, my idea is that this man who calls himself the Shadow has caused it to be known among the little sneak thieves, whizzers, and the servant classes that he's prepared to buy letters or documents that contain some disreputable secret concerning their owners. When any of these people get hold of such things they put one of these advertisements in the personal columns of a paper — they're all addressed to A. B. The Shadow communicates with them and arranges a time and place for an appointment.'

'It seems quite a feasible idea,' agreed Sir Richard. 'What are your plans for following it up?'

Elliot hesitated for a moment before replying. 'Well, sir,' he said at length, 'I propose to put an advertisement in tonight's *Evening News*, worded exactly the same as one of those, and if I'm lucky enough to get a reply, I shall keep the appointment. What do you think of the idea?'

'Quite a good one,' said the commissioner, nodding. 'But of course you won't go alone?'

'I shall, sir,' declared the superintendent. 'It might spoil everything if I had anyone with me, or trailing me. This man we're dealing with is clever and careful, and I've no doubt he takes infinite precautions. He must do, or we'd have had him before now.' He shook his head. 'No, sir, I shall go alone; that is, if I get the chance of keeping an appointment at all.'

He pushed back his chair and rose to his feet. 'Are there any suggestions you'd like to make, sir?' he asked respectfully, and for a long time Sir Richard remained silent, glowering at his blotting pad, his fingers playing nervously with a pencil.

'No, I don't think so, Elliot,' he said suddenly. 'You'll let me know, of course, directly you get a reply?'

The superintendent nodded. 'Yes, sir,' he said. 'And now if you'll excuse me, I'll go and see about the insertion of this advertisement.'

The chief commissioner looked thoughtfully after him as he left the office; then as the door closed softly, he gave a sigh and continued with his interrupted work.

* * *

The advertisement appeared that evening, but it was not until two nights later that there was any reply, and then Superintendent James Elliot saw in the personal column of the *Evening News* the following:

'E.J. — Poste Restante Charing Cross — A.B.'

The big man felt a little thrill of excitement as he read the short message. His theory had been correct, and with average luck this should lead him to the man who called himself the Shadow.

He took the precaution of not calling at the post office himself; he was a fairly well-known figure, his photograph having appeared several times in the newspapers, and somebody might be watching. The young constable who went brought the letter back to Elliot's lodgings. It was addressed:

'EJ. To be called for.'

As soon as the messenger had gone, Elliot ripped open the envelope and eagerly withdrew the single sheet of paper it contained. The letter began without preliminary:

'Be on the Portsmouth Road at twelve o'clock to-morrow Friday (night) where it runs past Putney Common, bringing with you what you have for sale. A car with one orange headlamp will pick you up.'

The letter was typewritten even to the signature, and was signed 'the Shadow'.

The night was wet and cold, for it was the middle of October, and Superintendent Elliot shivered as he walked slowly along the dark and lonely road. The overcoat he wore for the occasion was thin and shabby, and offered little protection from the biting blasts of icy wind that drove the rain into his face and went moaning away among the trees that clustered on either side. He was a little early for the appointment with the unknown, for it wanted ten minutes as yet to the hour. He had come by a circuitous route to avoid any possibility of being followed, though this was very unlikely, since there was nothing to connect him with the E.J. of the advertisement. In his pocket reposed a packet of letters carefully prepared for the occasion, and with them, which added to his confidence, the cold, hard bulk of an automatic pistol.

Elliot was an unimaginative man, stolid and phlegmatic, more dogged than brilliant, who had reached his present position by sheer hard work. And yet as he walked slowly along, his eyes searching the road ahead for the first sign of the car he was expecting, he felt an unaccustomed thrill. Tonight would see the end of a great deal of patient investigation, and should prove to be the last step towards the further promotion that he knew awaited him if he brought this case to a successful conclusion.

He looked at his watch. There were still a few minutes to go before midnight, and the Shadow might not be punctual. Concluding that he had gone far enough, he turned, thrust his hands deeper into his pockets, and began to retrace his steps.

He had gone about a hundred yards when faintly in the distance behind him he heard the purr of a car and, swinging round, saw dim headlights approaching. The one nearest the kerb was tinged faintly with orange, and his heart began to beat a little quicker. The lights drew swiftly nearer, and then the long, steaming bonnet of a small coupé ran past him and came to a halt. The window went down with a rattle, and a hard metallic voice said: 'E.J.?'

Elliot nodded. 'That's me,' he answered in a husky voice.

The door of the coupé was thrust open. 'Get in!' snapped the voice sharply, and stooping, Elliot insinuated his large bulk into the seat beside the driver.

'Close the door,' said the shadowy figure at his side, and as he pulled it shut the car started forward.

For a moment there was silence, and the superintendent took stock of his companion. He could not see very much of him, for he was wrapped in a heavy leather coat, the high collar of which was turned up and met the brim of the soft hat he was wearing. The hands on the wheel were gloved, and the face was covered by a dark handkerchief.

'What have you got?' asked the Shadow at last, as the car ran smoothly forward.

'Letters,' answered Elliot; he had prepared his story and began to tell it glibly. He had been chauffeur to Lord Brewer, but had been discharged. Quite without reason, he explained, although he hinted that he might have had a couple more than was good for him. He had heard that his companion bought letters of a spicy nature, and he had got some written to his employer by a certain little lady of whose existence Lady Brewer was unaware. He did not go into details as to how he had got possession of the letters, but made a vague reference to having been left alone in his employer's study on one occasion. He congratulated himself on having told the tale pretty well.

The driver of the car listened in silence until he had finished, and then he said: 'All right, I'll have a look at them.' He brought the machine to a halt at the side of the road, and a tiny light gleamed on the dashboard.

Elliot dived his hand into his pocket to bring out the packet of letters, and as he did so he felt something hard grind into his ribs.

'You did it very well, Superintendent Elliot,' said the mocking voice of the man beside him, 'but not well enough. Open that door and get out!'

The startled superintendent thought rapidly. So the other had seen through his subterfuge, and had merely been playing with him. His fingers closed round the butt of the pistol in his pocket, and he made a movement to draw it out.

'Keep still!' hissed the Shadow menacingly. 'If you don't, I'll put a bullet through you where you sit!' The hard muzzle of the automatic he held was pressed closer into Elliot's side to emphasize his words. 'Now open the door and get out!' the man repeated.

The superintendent obeyed, and the other followed him. The car had been stopped in a lonely and deserted portion of the road, where the trees of the surrounding common grew thickly to the edge of the sidewalk. The Shadow slipped his hand into Elliot's pocket and, taking out the pistol the superintendent carried, dropped it into his own. 'Now,' he said, 'walk over among those trees . . .'

Two minutes later, the Shadow returned to his car alone. The handkerchief no longer concealed his face, and his heavy motor coat was open, the buttonholes torn. He was panting heavily, and had to pause for a moment, leaning against the car, before he could regain his breath. Then he got in, slid behind the wheel and, reaching out, slammed the door. The car moved forward, gathered speed, and disappeared in the darkness of the deserted road.

At ten o'clock the next morning, a patrolling policeman discovered the dead body of Superintendent James Elliot lying among the bracken. He had been shot twice, and must have been dead for some time, for the blood which had soaked the front of his coat was dry and stiff.

4

The Charm

They found a little gold and platinum charm clutched in the dead man's hand. It was the only clue that the unknown murderer had left behind.

There were distinct signs of a struggle having taken place, and it was Chief Inspector Fleming's theory that the charm had been torn from the murderer's watch chain, for the ring at one end of it, which showed that it had originally been suspended from something, was broken.

Fleming, who had been sent to investigate the tragic death of his colleague, brought it back to Scotland Yard, and he and the chief commissioner examined it together in the latter's office on the afternoon following the murder.

'It's rather a distinctive thing, sir,' said the chief inspector, a tall, thin man with a large head and a face that was totally devoid of expression. 'It shouldn't be difficult to trace the jeweller from whom it was bought.'

Sir Richard regarded the little object that lay on his blotting pad and nodded. It was less than an inch in length, and the design was certainly uncommon — a golden hand holding in its crooked fingers a sphere of platinum. To the wrist was attached a tiny ring, and it had evidently been intended to hang from a chain or bracelet.

'Elliot must have snatched at it during the struggle with the idea of leaving behind a clue to the murderer's identity,' he remarked thoughtfully. 'This is the first time, by the way, that the Shadow has been guilty of actual murder.' He looked up at Fleming. 'He's been responsible for many deaths, but he's never killed in cold blood before.'

'I suppose there's no doubt that it *was* the Shadow who killed Elliot, sir,' said the chief inspector musingly, and the commissioner shook his head.

'I don't think there can be the slightest,' he replied, 'not after what Elliot told me yesterday morning. He had an appointment with the man. I wanted him to take Carr with him, or rather have him near at hand, but he wouldn't hear of it. He came in a car, didn't he? You found the tyre marks?'

Fleming nodded. 'Yes, we found the tyre marks,' he said softly. 'You refer to the Shadow as a man, sir. Has it ever occurred to you that it might be a woman?'

Sir Richard looked at him suddenly, a startled expression in his eyes. 'What do you mean?' he snapped.

'It's only a suggestion, of course, sir,' Fleming went on. 'But supposing that the Shadow is a woman — it would account to some extent for the fact that up to the present we've all been unsuccessful. What I mean is this. We've been so busy looking for a man that we've overlooked the possibility of it being a woman, and yet that charm — ' He made a gesture towards the tiny trinket. ' — is the sort of thing that a woman would wear.'

The commissioner pursed his lips. 'It seems hardly possible to me,' he said doubtfully. 'The brutality of this murder doesn't seem to fit with a woman at all.'

'Marie Hendrick killed her husband with a hammer,' put in the chief inspector quietly. 'Elizabeth Watts poisoned her son in order to get the insurance money, and I could give you a dozen other cases, sir.' He shook his head slowly. 'A woman is quite capable of doing all the things that have been attributed to the Shadow.'

A curious expression flitted across the troubled face of the commissioner, but it was gone in a second, and if Fleming had noticed it, he gave no sign. 'There may be something in what you say, Fleming,' he replied, 'but at present it doesn't help us. Whether the Shadow is a man or a woman, we're just as far from discovering his identity as when we started.'

'Not quite, sir,' the other disagreed. 'We've got the charm. Before, we hadn't any clue at all.'

Sir Richard inclined his head rather wearily. 'That's true,' he said, 'but it may not be of much use. There's no knowing where it was bought or when. It's obviously not new, and may have passed through several hands before it reached the person who killed Elliot.'

'Still, we can have a description circulated to all the jewellers in the country, sir,' said Fleming. 'There's a chance it might bring results.' With a sudden abrupt outburst of anger, he brought his clenched fist down on the palm of his left hand. 'If only we knew what Elliot knew!' he cried savagely, and with a quick movement rose to his feet. 'I'll get the Shadow, Chief; if it takes me ten years, I'll get him!'

Sir Richard looked at the burly figure radiating strength and energy, and for an instant his eyes clouded. 'Mind he doesn't get you first,' he said seriously, and throughout the rest of his busy day, the words kept recurring to Chief Inspector Fleming, causing him no little uneasiness. For there had been something prophetic in the manner of their utterance.

★ ★ ★

Later that same afternoon, two people sat on either side of a small table in a certain café within a stone's throw of Shaftesbury Avenue. A tray containing a teapot and two dirty cups had been pushed to one side, and the man had spread out on the space thus cleared a crumpled sheet of paper, and was occupied in drawing a rough plan in pencil. The woman watched him through narrowed eyes that spoke eloquently of short sight.

They were a striking couple, both fashionably dressed, and the woman was almost beautiful; almost, because the hardness about her mouth and the sophistication of her dark eyes detracted from a face that might otherwise have been entirely lovely. Her complexion was of that dead white that is sometimes the accompaniment of very dark hair; and although her lips had been touched with scarlet, she was without make-up. Her companion was also dark, with eyes that were set a shade too close to the large though well-shaped nose, and gave him an expression of shiftiness that spoilt an otherwise engaging personality.

'I think it's much too dangerous,' murmured the woman, as he finished his rough sketch and looked at it with satisfaction.

'Don't be absurd,' he answered impatiently. 'There's absolutely no danger at all if we follow the scheme I've outlined.'

'It's risky, I tell you,' she persisted.

He laughed, pulled out a thin gold cigarette case, selected a cigarette and, lighting it, flicked the used match neatly into an ashtray. 'You're losing your nerve, Moya, that's what's the matter with you,' he remarked contemptuously.

'I'm not.' She flushed in a sudden temper. 'I'm only trying to prevent you running your head into a noose.'

For a moment the man's face paled, and the hand holding the cigarette shook slightly. 'That's rather an unfortunate expression, isn't it, in the circumstances?' he said a trifle huskily.

She shrugged her shoulders and made a grimace. 'Perhaps it is,' she answered, 'but it's a very appropriate one.'

With an effort, he recovered from his momentary agitation. 'I can't see that there's the slightest chance of anything going wrong,' he argued. 'What could possibly happen?'

'Anything!' she retorted. 'However carefully you lay your plans, you can't allow for chance; that's going to beat you in the end. Just because you've been lucky up to now, it doesn't say you're always going to be.'

'And equally it doesn't say I'm not,' he answered.

'No, but each time the odds are greater.' She leaned forward across the table earnestly. 'Do you suppose they're *all* fools at Scotland Yard?'

His thick lips curled into a smile that showed even, white teeth. 'Certainly not,' he said. 'The cleaners, I believe, are most intelligent!'

She made a gesture of annoyance. 'You may think that's funny,' she snapped. 'I don't!'

'Your sense of humour was never very highly developed,' he murmured slowly, expelling a cloud of smoke.

'A sense of humour is not much good when they come to fetch you at eight o'clock in the morning,' she answered quickly, and the man winced.

'That's the second time you've made a remark that's not in the best of taste,' he said. 'I don't know what's come over you, Moya. You never used to suffer from nerves.'

'I'm not suffering from nerves now,' she said, shaking her head. 'I'm suffering from common sense, only you won't see it.' She stretched a gloved hand across the table and laid it gently on his arm. 'I wish you'd drop this idea,' she pleaded.

He frowned and shook his head stubbornly. 'I won't,' he answered emphatically. 'It's no good arguing. I've gone to too much trouble over the thing to draw back now. Apart from practically throwing away ten thousand pounds.'

Moya sighed and lifted one shoulder wearily. 'Well, you can't say I didn't warn you,' she muttered. 'When do we go?'

'On Saturday. I'll go through the whole plan again, and you can check it.' He crushed out the stub of his cigarette and, drawing his chair closer to the table, began talking swiftly in low tones while the woman listened, punctuating his sentences every now and again with a nod.

It was a clever scheme, but it was destined to have far-reaching results, and end in a way that was totally unexpected. For in the combination of circumstances they had allowed for, there was one element that neither of them had taken into consideration. And that was the weather!

5

At Green Lanes

The fog, which was destined to play such a large part in the events that were to come, descended upon London suddenly in the early hours of Saturday morning. By nine o'clock it was so thick that it was impossible to see more than a yard ahead. Traffic was reduced to almost a standstill, and the railway services were so disorganised as to be little more than useless.

Unfortunately it was not merely confined to the metropolis, but spread over a wide area, smothering the outlying districts in an impenetrable vapour. It was at its worst at Tatsfield, on the outskirts of which stood Green Lanes, Sir Richard Bryant's country home. It was so bad in this district that the chief commissioner, after communicating with the railway station, had been forced to telephone to Scotland Yard and inform the assistant commissioner that it was impossible for him to get up to town that day unless the fog lifted.

But the fog apparently had no intention of lifting; if anything, it got thicker and more ochre-coloured as the day advanced. The weather fitted in well with Sir Richard's own gloomy thoughts, and plunged him into a fit of the blackest depression.

A week had passed since Superintendent Elliot had died, struck down by the hand of the man whose identity he had been on the point of discovering; and during the intervening period, Fleming, working with a dogged persistence that was characteristic of the man, had left no stone unturned in order to try and trace the peculiarly shaped charm that had been found in the dead man's hand. All his efforts, however, were fruitless; and except for the fact that the Yard had lost one of its best men, they were no nearer to the Shadow than they had been before. He had appeared as an intangible shape out of the darkness of the night, delivered his death blow, and vanished again, unseen and unknown, a veritable phantom of destruction.

During the morning of that fatal Saturday, which was to become so eventful in the lives of the entire household, Sir Richard rambled about the big house restlessly, scarcely answering when he was spoken to, his mind obsessed with an unexplainable foreboding of impending disaster.

Lunch was an unusually silent meal, save for Reginald Stimpson's inane chatter; the voluble Mrs. Bascombe, suffering from one of her periodic headaches, having remained in bed. Afterward, Sir Richard locked himself in his study, and by a supreme effort of will tried to concentrate on some personal business matters that required his immediate attention.

Even Sonia, whose healthy, cheerful nature generally imparted an air of brightness throughout the house, was conscious of the electric tension in the atmosphere; and with the object of trying to dissipate the spirit of unrest that had communicated itself to her, she retired with a novel to the library. Curling herself up on the wide settee before the log fire, she tried to fix her attention upon the story.

It was a large, comfortable apartment, panelled in age-old oak that reflected the cheerful glow of the leaping flames and, in spite of the modern furniture, gave an air of the medieval to the whole room.

Green Lanes had been the home of the Bryants for generations. It was a rambling mansion of grey stone, built to withstand a siege, and set amidst many acres of wooded ground. The moat, which at one period of its existence had surrounded the old building, had long since been filled in. But the portcullis at the big arched main entrance still remained, though no longer usable.

Reginald Stimpson, who had followed Sonia — rather disconsolately, she thought — into the library, stood by one of the long windows, gazing silently out upon the yellow murk that obscured all vision. The son of an old friend of Sir Richard's, he had the run of the house; and although he possessed a flat somewhere in the vicinity of Piccadilly, he spent the greater part of his time at Tatsfield, where a room was always kept ready for him. He had become something of an institution, like the silver or the pictures, and would have been almost as acutely missed. For half an hour he remained silent by the window, staring vacantly at the curtain of fog.

'I say, it's fearfully foggy,' he remarked at length without turning.

Sonia looked up from her book. 'That's the third time since lunch you've said that,' she answered wearily. 'Can't you think of anything else?'

'Well, it's true,' he protested.

She laid aside her book and sat watching the crackling logs through half-closed eyes. 'You'll have to cultivate more imagination if you want to become a popular author,' she said.

'But I've got an awfully vivid imagination, really, old thing.' He left the window and came over to the wide fireplace. 'I've just thought out a perfectly priceless plot for a thriller. The fog gave me the idea.'

'Most of your ideas come from fog,' she commented dryly.

'But this is really tophole,' he continued. 'The best I've ever struck. I'll tell you. Listen. A johnny gets lost in the fog and can't find his way — '

'Of course he can't, if he's lost,' she interrupted, but the enthusiastic author was not to be put off.

'He's miles away from anywhere,' he went on, 'and all of a sudden he comes across a lonely cottage, all by itself. He goes up the path, and stumbles over something.' He paused, lowering his voice impressively. 'He strikes a match, and finds that it's a dead body!'

Sonia shifted the cushion until she was more comfortable. 'Well?' she said, suppressing a yawn.

'Of course, the poor old blighter gets a fearful shock, finding things like that about the place, you know. But there's worse to come.' He began walking back and forth in his excitement. 'The cottage door is open, and in the passage he finds another body. He begins to think by now that something's happened, you know — '

'Naturally!' said Sonia sarcastically.

'But that isn't all. He explores further — and what do you think he finds?' He stopped and blinked at her expectantly.

'How should I know?' she said, looking round at him. 'Another body?'

Yes,' he said, nodding. 'You've got the idea — bodies all over the place! One in every room, and the whole point of the thing is, no one knows who killed them.'

'Well, who did kill them?' she asked, since he obviously expected her to say something.

'Eh?' He stared at her a little blankly, and she repeated her question. 'I haven't got as far as that, old thing,' he answered, shaking his head and returning to the fireplace. 'I've got to work that out.'

'I think it's a perfectly rotten story,' she said, uncurling her legs and sitting up. 'What's the time? I'm dying for some tea.'

'It's a quarter to four,' he answered, peering at the clock on the mantelpiece. There was a short silence during which he looked at Sonia, dimly visible in the glow from the fire, a trifle uncertainly. At last, suddenly making up his mind, he leaned forward.

'I say, old thing,' he began nervously, 'there's, er, something I want to say to you, and this seems rather a priceless opportunity, what?'

She raised her eyes in astonishment at his serious tone and opened her lips to speak, but he went rushing on.

'You see, I've sort of known you for a long time, and you've known me almost as long, as it were, and I've been wondering, er, if . . . er, that is . . . ' His voice trailed away incoherently.

'For heaven's sake, don't stutter, it's a shockingly bad habit,' she said.

'I'm not stuttering,' he protested. 'I'm merely trying to clothe the thought with words suitable to the occasion.'

'Well, go on,' she replied a little impatiently.

'I will,' he said, nodding vehemently. 'What I'm trying to say is, er . . . couldn't we . . . er, fix up some sort of a collaboration?'

'Do you want me to help you with your

stories?' asked Sonia in bewilderment as he stopped.

'No, no, nothing of the kind, old thing,' he replied hastily. 'You see, it's like this.' He drew a long breath. 'I'm, er, awfully fond of you, and all that bally rot, and I was wondering if we couldn't, er, hitch up together, and — '

'Reggie!' she exclaimed as his meaning suddenly dawned on her. 'Are you trying to propose?'

'Yes, that's it,' he said with evident relief. 'It's jolly difficult.'

'It's impossible!' she answered quickly.

'Oh no, it's not impossible,' he disagreed. 'It only requires a little willpower, you know!'

She laughed. 'I didn't mean that,' she explained. 'I meant, I could never marry you.'

'Oh, I'm sure you could if you tried,' he spoke hurriedly, stumbling over his words. 'I'm serious, really I am. Awfully serious.'

'I'm afraid it's impossible,' she said. 'I like you, but not in that way.'

He looked very disconsolate. 'It's pretty

hopeless, then, and all that, what?' he said.

'Quite,' she answered, and his expression was so forlorn that she stretched out her hand impulsively. 'I'm terribly sorry.'

'Oh, don't trouble to apologise, old dear.' He took her hand for a moment gingerly, and then dropped it as though it were a hot coal. 'It was only an idea of mine, that's all. I won't mention it again.'

He strolled over to the window, and there followed a rather strained silence. The entrance of Willit, the butler, with tea served to put an end to a rather embarrassing situation, and Sonia welcomed him with something approaching a prayer of thankfulness.

'Shall I put the lights on, miss?' asked the grey-haired butler, setting the silver tray he was carrying down on a small table at the head of the settee.

'Yes, please, Willit.' She rose and smoothed her skirt. 'Where's Father?'

'Sir Richard is in his study, miss,' replied Willit, switching on the light and pulling the curtains over the windows. 'I've already told him that tea is served.'

'And Mrs. Bascombe?' asked Sonia.

'In her room, miss. She said she would be down directly. Is there anything else, miss?'

She glanced quickly over the laden tray and shook her head. 'No, thank you, Willit.'

The butler bowed and withdrew, and she looked after him thoughtfully. 'Have you noticed any difference lately in Willit?' she asked suddenly.

Stimpson, who had lighted a cigarette and was glancing through a magazine, put it down and stared at her in astonishment. 'Difference?' he echoed blankly. 'Don't understand you, old thing.'

'Perhaps it's only my imagination after all,' she answered with a slight frown, 'but he looks changed; as though he had something on his mind.'

He took a silk handkerchief from his pocket and polished his monocle vigorously. 'Perhaps he's coming down with a cold or something,' he suggested.

'Nonsense!' she said with an impatient gesture. 'That wouldn't make him look like he does.'

Stimpson screwed his eyeglass carefully into his right eye. 'How does he look?' he asked.

'Frightened,' she answered slowly. 'That's the only way I can describe it — frightened.'

'I say, this is jolly interesting,' exclaimed Stimpson. 'Like one of my bally stories, what?'

'They're not interesting!' she retorted coolly. 'But seriously, Reggie, I'm rather concerned about Willit. I'm sure there's something wrong — '

She broke off as the door opened suddenly, and a woman tripped gaily into the room. She was small and thin, with a mass of remarkably coloured hair that had certainly never drawn its redness from nature; and her age would undoubtedly have been set down in an algebraic problem under the equation X.

'I hope I haven't kept you waiting, darling,' she exclaimed in a high coquettish treble, and without pausing to even punctuate her sentences, 'but my poor head was so terribly bad that I simply couldn't get up. Where is dear Sir Richard?'

'In the study,' answered Sonia, beginning to pour out the tea. 'Reggie, be a dear and go and tell him that tea's ready.'

'Certainly, old thing.'

That obliging young man hurried off on his errand, and Mrs. Bascombe fluttered into a chair by the fire with a little sigh. 'Poor, dear Sir Richard,' she remarked sympathetically. 'He's been looking so ill lately. I suppose the care of all those policemen must be a great load on his mind. There's something so attractive about the uniform, dear, don't you think? I always did like blue. So heavenly.'

'There's nothing very heavenly about a policeman,' said Sonia, handing her a cup of tea.

'No?' Mrs. Bascombe seemed mildly surprised. 'Perhaps not, but they're such a brave body of men. I always used to say to poor, dear George how wonderful it is to think that when one is in bed and asleep, they are watching to protect one from burglars and horrid people like that who take things that don't belong to them. I'm terribly afraid of burglars, darling, aren't you? I always look under the bed every night before putting out the light. Not that I've ever found anyone, but — '

'You've never quite lost hope, eh?'

Mrs. Bascombe gave a little affected scream and looked up at Sir Richard, who had entered silently while she was speaking and was standing behind her chair.

'Oh, Sir Richard, you naughty man!' she cried, shaking a finger at him archly. 'Whatever do you mean? If I ever saw a burglar, I think I should die!'

'There are worse people in the world than burglars, Mrs. Bascombe,' said the chief commissioner gravely.

'Worse than burglars?' She raised carefully painted eyebrows. 'What could be worse?'

Sir Richard shrugged his shoulders and stirred his tea. 'The Shadow,' he replied.

'How's the old joker getting on?' asked Stimpson. 'Have you discovered anything further about him?'

The chief commissioner shook his

head. 'No,' he replied, 'nothing. Since the murder of poor Elliot we've been at a deadlock.'

'You'll have to let me have a shot,' remarked Reggie. 'You'll never catch this fellow without my help. You're absolutely out of your depth, what? I know all about these chappies; I write stories about 'em.'

'Unfortunately they don't behave in real life as they do in stories,' replied Sir Richard.

'Oh, but they do,' protested Stimpson. 'They must, old boy. You can't have a criminal without clues, any more than you can have clues without a criminal. Now this Shadow johnny — he must have left some sort of a clue.'

'He did,' began Sir Richard, 'but — '

'There you are!' exclaimed the other triumphantly. 'My dear old lad, doesn't that prove I'm right?'

'But it hasn't proved of much use up to now,' the chief commissioner concluded.

'What was it?' asked Sonia, pausing in the act of sipping her tea.

'I don't know that I ought to tell you police secrets, child,' said Sir Richard, looking at her with a smile. 'But I don't see that it can do any harm. It was a little gold and platinum charm, a clenched hand holding a sphere — Good heavens, what's the matter, my dear?'

There was a crash of broken china as the cup and saucer slipped from Sonia's nerveless fingers and smashed to pieces on the floor at her feet!

6

The Man Who Came In

White-faced and trembling, Sonia rose unsteadily to her feet.

'What's the matter?' repeated the chief commissioner anxiously. 'Are you feeling ill?'

She shook her head and forced a laugh, but it was not a very successful attempt. 'No, no, I'm all right,' she answered in a low voice. 'Just my clumsiness; the cup slipped. I'll ring for Willit to clear up the mess.'

She turned to the fireplace and pressed the bell. The action served to hide the peculiar expression that had crept into her eyes, an expression in which fear and doubt were curiously mingled. When she again faced the others, it was gone, and she was almost normal. 'You were saying something about a charm?' she said questioningly.

Sir Richard crossed over to the writing table and searched for a cigarette. 'Yes,' he said, helping himself from the silver box and lighting it from the little table lighter. 'It was found in Elliot's hand. Chief Inspector Fleming has been trying to trace the jeweller from whom it was bought. So far, I'm sorry to say, without success.'

'Is this trinket thing supposed to belong to the Shadow?' asked Stimpson, languidly setting his empty cup down on the tray.

'Almost certainly,' replied the chief commissioner. He was about to say something more, but at that moment Willit entered in answer to Sonia's ring, and he remained silent. He strolled over to the window and, pulling aside the curtains, stared thoughtfully out.

'I'm afraid I've spoilt the rug, Willit,' said Sonia as the old butler bent down and began clearing up the broken pieces of china.

While he was so engaged, the telephone rang suddenly. Sir Richard, who was over by the desk, picked up the receiver.

'Hello? Yes, this is Green Lanes. Speaking.' He paused, listening to the almost inaudible voice of the man at the other end of the wire. 'Who's that? Who?' He frowned and shook his head.

'I'm sorry, but I can't understand what you're saying. There must be something the matter with this line. Who are you? Oh, Fleming.' Again he paused, and Sonia, watching him closely, saw his face suddenly change. His mouth hardened and grew tense. 'What's that?' he went on sharply. 'Hello? Hello?' He banged the instrument irritably. 'Damn the thing — they've cut us off!'

He tried vainly to get into communication again with the speaker, for Fleming's voice had suddenly died away to silence amid a faint spluttering and crackling. At last, with an impatient exclamation, he banged the receiver back on the hook, and turned to Sonia. 'This line must be out of order,' he said with a frown of annoyance. 'I can't even get any reply from the exchange now. That was Fleming phoning from Oxted station. He managed to get down by train. I couldn't hear half of what he said, but he's coming along here as soon as he can.'

'It must have been something urgent to have brought him down here on a day like this,' she said.

Sir Richard nodded. 'It is,' he answered crisply. 'Very urgent. From what I can gather, he's on the track of the Shadow.'

Stimpson turned swiftly from the window. 'By jove!' he exclaimed excitedly. 'You don't mean that he's found out who the old johnny is?'

'That's what he said.' The chief commissioner drummed with his fingers on the table impatiently. 'He was just going to tell me when the phone went wrong. I wonder — '

What he wondered they never knew, for at that moment Mrs. Bascombe suddenly gave a piercing scream and pointed a shaking finger at the window. 'Look! Look!' she cried hysterically. 'There's a man outside peering in!'

They swung round, following the direction of her shaking hand, but they saw nothing.

'There's no one there,' said Sonia

soothingly. 'You're imagining things.'

'I'm not,' declared the older woman brokenly. 'I saw a face, a horrible face, pressed close to the glass.'

'Some trick of the light, I expect,' said Sir Richard. 'It couldn't have been anyone.'

'I'm jolly well going to have a look,' cried Stimpson excitedly. 'By jove, it might have been the old Shadow himself!'

'Don't talk nonsense!' said the chief commissioner impatiently. 'The Shadow's not likely to be down here.'

'You don't know where the old bean is,' answered Stimpson, unlatching the window. 'If he isn't somewhere down here, why should Fleming have come down?' He vanished into a swirling cloud of yellow fog, pulling the window to after him.

'I'm sure it was the face of a desperate criminal!' wailed Mrs. Bascombe, who had reached the sobbing stage. 'He hadn't shaved for days!'

'I know a lot of men who haven't shaved for years, but they're not desperate criminals,' snapped Sir Richard. 'If it was anyone at all, it was probably only some unfortunate tramp.'

'You don't think it could have been the Shadow?' Sonia spoke huskily, a queer look in her eyes.

'Of course not, my dear,' he answered. 'It's only one of Reggie's stupid ideas. Why should the Shadow be wandering about my grounds in the fog?'

Before his daughter could reply, Stimpson re-entered, smiling cheerfully. 'No one there,' he announced. 'Absolutely no one at all. Not even the ghost of a Shadow, what?'

The commissioner, who had put his arm round Sonia's shoulders, felt her shiver slightly, and looked at her with alarm. 'Why, child, what's the matter?' he asked. 'You're trembling.'

'I can't help it,' she confessed. 'It's stupid, I know, but all this talk about the Shadow, and then Alicia seeing someone looking in — I feel frightened!'

Sir Richard patted her arm affectionately. 'There's nothing to be frightened about,' he said reassuringly. 'Mrs. Bascombe imagined the whole thing.'

'I didn't!' broke in that lady sharply. 'I saw an awful face.'

'Of course,' said Stimpson suddenly. 'I know, you must have seen your own!'

'Mr. Stimpson!' Mrs. Bascombe's tone was awful in its righteous indignation, and the unfortunate Stimpson wilted under her ferocious glare.

'I, er, I didn't exactly mean that, you know,' he stammered in confusion. 'What I meant was, it must have been your reflection in the glass of the jolly old window that you mistook for a face.'

'Good gracious!' cried the offended lady, relapsing into tears. 'I've suffered enough with the shock without you insulting me.'

'I'm awfully sorry if I said anything to annoy you, he began, but she refused to listen to his apologies. Stifling her sobs, she rose to her feet and swept to the door.

'You haven't annoyed me, you've hurt me,' she said, pausing on the threshold. 'I shall have to go upstairs and lie down. I wish I'd never seen the wretched face. But when we're all murdered in our beds, you'll thank me!' She went out, slamming the door behind her, and Stimpson stared at the others in comical dismay.

'Would you believe it possible that a woman of her age could be so foolish?' exclaimed the commissioner angrily.

'Do you really think she saw anything?' asked Sonia.

He shook his head quickly. 'No, pure imagination,' he replied.

'If she did, I must have missed him in the mist,' said Stimpson lightly. He chuckled feebly. 'I say, that's jolly good, what?' He looked from one to the other for some sign of appreciation.

Sonia stamped her foot in sudden anger. 'I do wish you wouldn't keep joking!' she cried. 'I've a feeling that something's going to happen.'

'What do you mean, child?' asked Sir Richard seriously.

She rested her elbow on the mantelpiece and looked down into the fire. 'I don't know,' she said after a pause, speaking in such a low voice that they found difficulty in hearing what she said. 'I can't explain. It's just a feeling, that's all.' She raised her head suddenly. 'Do you remember when I was quite small and my little dog, Tatters, was run over and killed?' Sir Richard nodded. 'I knew he was going to be killed long before it actually happened,' she went on quickly. 'Well, I've got the same feeling now. Somewhere round this house is something evil, something horrible.' She stopped abruptly, and Stimpson uneasily stroked the back of his neck.

'I say, old thing,' he exclaimed, 'you're giving me the creeps!'

'It's nerves, Sunny,' said the chief commissioner, coming to her side and putting his arm round her. 'That confounded woman has upset you.'

'No, no, it's not Alicia,' she answered, shaking her head. 'I've felt the same all day. I've tried to put it out of my mind, but it's there, behind everything I do and say. I've only experienced the same feeling once before in my life, when my little dog was killed.'

Whatever comment Sir Richard was going to make got no further than his lips, for the entrance of Willit made him turn towards the door with the words unuttered. The grey-haired butler was standing nervously on the threshold. 'There's a lady and gentleman in the hall, sir,' he announced.

The chief commissioner raised his eyebrows in astonishment. 'A lady and gentleman?' he repeated in surprise. 'Who are they?'

The butler shook his head slowly. 'I don't know, sir,' he answered. 'The gentleman says his name is Silverton, and that his car has broken down. He wants to know if you would be so kind as to allow him to use the telephone, sir.'

'I'm afraid that's impossible, Willit,' said Sir Richard. 'Something appears to have gone wrong with the line.'

The butler bowed and was turning away, when his master stopped him with a gesture. 'Wait,' he said. 'What sort of people are they?'

Willit hesitated. 'He seems almost a gentleman, sir,' he answered after a slight pause.

'By jove! Billy Bennett!' exclaimed the irrepressible Stimpson.

The chief commissioner motioned him

to be quiet. 'What do you mean by that?' he asked, addressing Willit.

'Well, he's very nicely dressed, sir,' answered the butler.

'And what about the lady?' enquired Sonia.

'She is — well, very modern, miss,' said Willit, and his tone expressed his disapproval.

'Nicely undressed, I suppose,' chuckled Stimpson, and Sonia laughed.

'Really, Reggie,' she remarked, 'that's quite clever for you!'

'You'd better ask them in,' said Sir Richard, rubbing his chin; and when the butler had gone: 'We can hardly do less than ask these people in, I suppose, whoever they are. They can't wander about in this foul weather. Where are you going?' he added as Reggie walked over to the window.

'Just to have a look round,' said Stimpson airily, 'in case there happens to be anyone hanging about the house who shouldn't be hanging about the house, what! If I don't come back for dinner, you can dig up the moat.' He laughed and disappeared into the fog.

'Young idiot!' growled Sir Richard. 'All he'll ever succeed in catching is a cold.'

The door opened as he spoke and Willit ushered in the newcomers. The man was of middle height, dressed in a leather motor coat and carrying a cap in his gloved hands. He was dark, with carefully brushed hair that gleamed with brilliantine, and his face would have been handsome but for the eyes, which were set too close to the nose. The woman who followed him was tall, and walked with the affected swing of the professional mannequin. Her large, dark eyes darted swiftly about her and took in every detail of her surroundings.

The man advanced towards Sir Richard with a pleasant smile that showed his white, even teeth. 'I'm most awfully sorry to disturb you like this,' he apologised, 'but I explained the situation to your butler. Unfortunately my car has broken down, and I thought perhaps you would be kind enough to allow me to phone the nearest garage and hire another.'

'I should be only too pleased, Mr., er,

er, Silverton,' said Sir Richard courteously. 'But, like your car, my telephone has also broken down.'

'By jove!' exclaimed Silverton. 'That is hard luck!' He pursed his rather thick lips. 'Perhaps you wouldn't mind if my sister stopped here while I went to the garage?'

'The nearest garage is over four miles away,' replied the chief commissioner, 'and you'd never find your way in this fog. However, if you care to stay until the fog clears, I'll send a groom down for you, or doubtless my own chauffeur could put your car right in the meanwhile.'

'It's really very kind of you.' Silverton paused and looked at the other questioningly. 'I'm afraid I haven't the pleasure of knowing whom I am addressing.'

'My name is Bryant,' said Sir Richard. 'Richard Bryant.'

The woman uttered a faint sound and swayed, clutching at a corner of a chair for support, and beneath the make-up her face had gone suddenly grey. Sonia stepped forward quickly and led her to a chair.

'What's the matter?' she asked in concern. 'Are you feeling ill?'

With an obvious effort the woman recovered her self-control. 'No, no, I'm all right now, thank you,' she muttered huskily. 'I felt a little faint for a moment, that's all.'

The fur coat she was wearing was soaked with moisture, and her gloveless hands were blue with cold. 'You'd better come with me and change your things,' suggested Sonia. 'You're wet through.'

She took the unwilling woman to the door, and when they had gone Silverton turned to Sir Richard. 'My sister hasn't been feeling very well all day,' he remarked. 'I'm afraid she's caught a chill.'

'My daughter will look after her,' said his host. 'Probably you'd care for something to take the taste of the fog away, eh?' He pressed the bell.

'Thanks very much. Yes, I should.' The dark man began to divest himself of his leather coat. 'I still feel rather guilty for having inflicted myself on you like this.'

'Not at all,' answered Sir Richard. 'Oh, Willit — ' He turned to the butler, who had entered softly. ' — take some whisky into the smoking room, and show Chief Inspector Fleming in here as soon as he arrives.'

'Fleming?' Silverton was in the act of removing a gold cigarette case from the pocket of his motor coat; at the mention of the name it fell from his fingers with a clatter.

Sir Richard looked at him keenly. 'Do you know Fleming?' he asked sharply.

For a moment the man appeared confused, but he quickly recovered himself. 'No,' he replied, laughing, and stooped to pick up the cigarette case. 'The name rather startled me for a moment, that's all. My, er, sister's engaged to a man named Fleming.'

'Well, it can't be the same man,' chuckled the chief commissioner, conducting his visitor to the door, 'unless the chief inspector is contemplating bigamy!'

Willit watched them go, and his subsequent proceedings would have interested Sir Richard had he been there to see them. The butler crossed swiftly to the door and listened intently, and then with a quick jerk of his hand switched off the lights. He waited for a moment or two, straining his ears to catch the slightest sound of anyone returning, ready with his hand on the switch. But there was no such sound, and presently, stepping noiselessly, he went over to the window, opened it, and whistled twice softly. A muffled figure emerged from the wall of fog, and the butler grasped it by the arm.

'Come in, quick!' he whispered hoarsely, dragging the other into the room and closing the window. 'I'll get the sack if I'm caught, you know that.'

He hastily fastened the catch and hurriedly led the newcomer over to a door on the opposite side of the room. 'This way,' he continued in the same low tone, and opened the door. 'There's a cupboard just along the passage; you can hide there. It's dark, but you can feel for it. I've left the key on the inside. Lock yourself in and stay there until I give you the wire. Hurry — someone may come in at any moment.'

He pushed the muffled figure across the threshold and closed the door. When he switched on the lights again, his face was pale and dotted with little glistening drops of perspiration. And there was cause for his perturbation, for he had let into the house a desperate man whose one thought was his own safety, cost what it might. And in this, he had acted under a force stronger than his own will.

7

The Death Shot!

Alicia Bascombe was the type of woman who saw all men through the magic circle of a wedding ring, and age had not withered nor custom staled this intriguing if, to her, rather profitless pastime.

She had been a distant cousin — so many times removed that the relationship was in danger of disappearing altogether — of Sir Richard's wife; and on the death of her husband, a meek little man who had died from sheer lack of personality, she had one memorable day arrived at Green Lanes ostensibly on a short visit of condolence for Sir Richard's bereavement. The stay had, however, in some miraculous manner become elastic, and almost without it being realised she had become a fixed and immovable member of the household.

She possessed a microscopic allowance

that enabled her to buy such personal belongings as she required. And since Sir Richard had never made any objection to her remaining, she had seized the golden opportunity of acquiring a comfortable, even luxurious home, free of rental. Certainly in return she had acted in the capacity of a sort of companion to Sonia, who at that time had been a growing schoolgirl; and it was possibly for this reason that the chief commissioner had allowed, if not exactly welcomed, her presence in his establishment.

It was not due to any lack of encouragement on Mrs. Bascombe's part that she was not something more than a guest at Green Lanes; for she had almost from the first tried by every artifice in her power to entrap Sir Richard into a proposal. Indeed, even after years of failure, so optimistic was her nature that she still indulged in dreams of one day becoming mistress of the old mansion, and substituting 'Lady' for 'Mrs.' But this did not prevent her from trying to run several sidelines; and no male, from the vicar to the postman, was safe from her rather lavish attentions.

When, therefore, through the medium of Janet, Sonia's maid, she learned that a stranger had arrived, she proceeded with the greatest care to prepare herself in all her war paint for the fresh world that Providence had sent for her to conquer. Could she have heard the conversation that was at that precise moment taking place in the library below, her enthusiasm would possibly have been slightly dampened.

The dark woman who had accompanied Silverton was standing before the fire, gazing with a frowning stare at the red embers. She had changed her clothes and was dressed in a frock of Sonia's, which fitted her remarkably well considering the difference in their heights. Her brows were drawn together in deep thought, so that she failed to hear the door open softly, and the man who entered was almost beside her before she realised that she was no longer alone.

'Oh, it's you, is it,' she said with a sigh of relief. 'You startled me for a moment.'

Silverton seated himself on the arm of

the settee. 'I was hoping to catch you alone, Moya,' he said, speaking in a whisper. 'I saw you come down through the study door. Where's the daughter?'

'I left her upstairs,' she replied. 'Sir Richard was speaking to her.'

'Oh, that's where he went, is it.' He nodded with satisfaction. 'Perhaps we shan't be disturbed for a moment. Listen to me. The position's serious.'

Moya looked startled. 'What's happened?' she asked quickly. 'Does the old man suspect anything?'

Her companion shook his head with a sudden jerky movement. 'No, why should he?' he snapped. 'To hell with him! I'm not afraid of him, although I'll admit it gave me a bit of a shock when I realised who he was.' He rose to his feet and came closer to her side. 'Do you know who's expected here this evening?'

'No, who?' she asked.

'Fleming.' He grated the word through clenched teeth, and if she had looked startled before, her expression was now one of stark terror.

'Fleming?' she gasped. 'Coming here?'

He nodded shortly. 'Yes, I thought that would concern you,' he answered.

She grasped his arm tightly, her face a curious mottled grey. 'We must get away at once,' she began, but he shook off her hand and stopped her.

'That's easily said, but not so easily done! It's thicker than ever outside. We're three miles from the station, and anyway, I don't suppose there are any trains running,'

She bit her lip and frowned. 'Isn't there a hotel we could go to?' she suggested.

'There's not another house for miles,' he replied.

'We must do something,' she said quickly. 'I'd rather walk about in the fog all night than risk meeting Fleming.'

Her companion laughed harshly. 'I daresay you would,' he sneered. 'But do you realise what we should look like by the morning? Even a policeman would pinch us on sight.'

She passed the tip of her tongue across lips that had suddenly become dry and hard. 'Well, what can we do?' she said desperately.

'Nothing, except stay here.' He took a turn up and down the room and came back to her. 'If we tried to leave now it would arouse suspicion, and that's what we want to avoid.'

'But what about Fleming?' she urged. 'If he sees you — '

'Leave Fleming to me. I'll deal with him.' His voice was hard and menacing. 'If only this damned fog would clear, we could get away in one of the old man's cars.' He gave a short laugh. 'It would be rather funny to steal a car from the chief commissioner of Scotland Yard.'

'I'm laughing so much, I can't see the joke,' said his companion sarcastically, and then in a changed tone: 'Why is Fleming coming here at all? Do you think he . . . knows?'

'No, I've covered my tracks too well,' he answered. 'It must be just a coincidence.'

'Supposing it isn't?' she said, eyeing him steadily. 'Supposing he's after you?'

He returned her gaze for a moment, and then slipping his hand into his hip pocket, he took out a small automatic and balanced it on his palm. 'If that is the case,' he replied slowly, 'it will be very unpleasant for Fleming.'

Moya shrank back, one hand at her lips. 'You wouldn't,' she whispered huskily. 'Not — again?'

His lips curled back in a mirthless grin, and he re-pocketed the weapon. 'I would if it was necessary,' he muttered. 'It means a little walk at eight o'clock in the morning for me if I'm caught, and I hate getting up early.'

'Surely there's some other way than that,' she said.

'Oh, it would only be a last resort,' he answered, and although he spoke lightly, his voice held a grim undercurrent. 'I've got a fairly good idea of the ground plan of the house, which may be quite useful. We might have to leave in a hurry.' He pulled out his cigarette case with nervous fingers, lighted a cigarette, and let his eyes rove restlessly round the room. 'While we're here it wouldn't be a bad idea to leave these windows unlatched,' he remarked. 'It might save time when — Who the devil?'

He started back with a muttered oath, for he had barely raised the latch when the window was pushed open from outside, and a figure entered.

'Thanks awfully, old chappie,' said Reginald Stimpson, shivering with cold but wearing a cheerful grin. 'Jolly good of you! Saved me taking a little walk round to the front door, what?'

Silverton regarded him suspiciously. 'Who are you?' he demanded.

The would-be author of thrillers beamed at him and lighted a cigarette. 'My name's Stimpson, old boy,' he said pleasantly. 'Reginald Stimpson. I'm an author — write stories, you know, full of criminals and detectives and bodies, and odds and ends like that! They're jolly good, awfully good. I can't understand why the publishers always send 'em back.' He looked from one to the other with interest. 'I suppose you two are the stranded motorists, eh? Fearfully hard lines, what?'

Silverton listened impatiently, his face still dark with suspicion. 'What were you doing out there?' he demanded abruptly.

Stimpson looked at him through his monocle in mild surprise. 'Just admiring the view, old boy,' he replied innocently.

'In the fog?' said the girl sarcastically, and he nodded.

'Yes, I always think it looks better that way,' he remarked. He glanced at his watch and strolled over to the door. 'I think I'll just toddle off and get a bath. I often do that.' He paused on the threshold and looked back at Silverton. 'You ought to try one now and again, old thing,' he added, and went out, shutting the door behind him.

For a moment the man and the woman remained silent, and then it was she who spoke first. 'I wonder if he heard anything?' she said half-fearfully.

Silverton shrugged his shoulders contemptuously. 'No,' he replied. 'And even if he did, he's too much of a fool to understand.'

'All the same, I'd like to know what he was doing outside that window,' she muttered, and her hands were unsteady.

'For God's sake, don't get nervy,' snapped Silverton, his eyes narrowing. 'If you — ' He broke off sharply as the sound of voices came from the direction of the hall.

'Come into the library, Chief Inspector,' said the deep voice of a man. 'I don't know how you feel, but I'm nearly frozen.'

'So am I,' was the answer. 'Beastly weather!'

'That's Fleming,' grunted Silverton; and, seizing Moya by the arm, he dragged her over to the other door on the opposite side of the room. 'Come on, this way!' He jerked it open and hustled her through, closing it behind him just as Chief Inspector Fleming and a dark-haired, slim young man entered from the hall.

Fleming was clad in a huge overcoat, which added to his large bulk. Going straight over to the fire, he stooped and warmed his frozen hands. 'Lucky for us we met you, Mr. Kent,' he said over one shoulder. 'It would have taken us hours groping our way in this infernal fog. Where's Sir Richard?'

Beverley Kent, the chief commissioner's private secretary, stripped off his fur driving gloves. 'In the study, I expect,' he answered. 'I'll tell him you're here.'

'Thanks,' growled the inspector, and then as the other reached the door: 'Don't let anyone else in the house know I'm here. I don't want my presence advertised yet.'

The secretary looked at him curiously. 'What's in the wind?' he asked. 'Surely you can tell me. I'm in Sir Richard's confidence.'

The big man swung round sharply. 'You may be,' he snapped, 'but that doesn't say you're in mine. I don't wish to be rude, but I've learnt the value of keeping my mouth shut.'

'That must be nice for your wife,' said Kent with a chuckle, and went out.

Fleming glared at the closed door, and went on warming his hands by the fire. A moment later Sir Richard entered hastily. 'So you managed to find your way all right, in spite of the fog,' he greeted his visitor, shaking his outstretched hand.

Fleming nodded. 'Your secretary brought us along in the car, sir,' he said. 'He overtook us just outside the station.'

The commissioner raised his eyebrows questioningly. 'Us?' he repeated, and Fleming nodded again.

'Yes,' he replied, 'I've brought Carr and two plainclothes men with me. I've got them stationed outside now, watching all the exits to this house. They've orders to let no one leave.' He paused and looked the other straight in the face. 'Not even you, sir!' he added curtly.

'Good God!' exclaimed the commissioner in a startled tone. 'Why these precautions?'

The chief inspector took a step towards him. 'Listen,' he said impressively, 'when Elliot was killed and I took charge of this case, I told you I'd get the Shadow — and I have.' He opened and closed a huge hand. 'Like that! I've found the jeweller who sold that charm, and I've also found the person who bought it. You know him as well as I do.'

'I know him?' cried Sir Richard incredulously.

The other thrust his large face forward truculently. 'Yes. The person who bought that charm is here.'

'Here?' The chief commissioner looked at Fleming as though he had suddenly taken leave of his senses.

'In this house now!'

His superior frowned. 'Nonsense, Fleming,' he said. 'You've made a mistake. How — '

'I've made no mistake, sir,' interrupted the chief inspector. 'The Shadow is here.'

'Then who is he?' demanded Sir Richard sharply.

Fleming leaned forward, and neither Silverton nor Moya saw the door through which they had made their hasty exit open slowly, or the black-gloved hand that was seeking for the light switch.

'You're going to get the biggest surprise of your life, sir,' said the chief inspector grimly — and at that moment all the lights went out.

'Good God!' cried Sir Richard. 'What — '

A sharp report drowned the rest of his sentence, followed immediately by a strangled cry and the sound of a heavy fall. In the darkness Sir Richard felt something brush against him, and stretched out his hand, but his groping fingers closed on empty air.

'Fleming!' he cried. 'What's happened?'

But there was no reply. The air was heavy with the acrid smell of burnt cordite, which caught at his throat and set him coughing. Blundering to the light switch, he pressed it down, and as the room became flooded with light he drew in his breath with a sharp gasp of horror.

Crumpled up on the floor lay Fleming, his eyes open and staring, blood trickling sluggishly from a small round wound in his forehead. And it did not need a second glance to know that he was dead. He had known the Shadow, and because of his knowledge he had died, as Elliot had died, carrying the unspoken name with him to the grave!

8

Inspector Carr Takes Charge

The sound of the shot had been heard all over the house, and rapid footsteps were approaching the library door. It was flung violently open, and Beverley Kent appeared on the threshold, alarm written all over his good-looking face.

'What was that noise, Sir Richard?' he cried excitedly. 'What's the matter?'

The chief commissioner knelt down beside the body. 'Come here, Kent, quickly!' he said, striving to keep his voice steady. 'A terrible thing has happened. Fleming has been shot.'

'Shot?' The secretary's face went white and he hurried forward, staring down at the crumpled figure on the floor with horrified eyes. 'How did it happen? Who shot him?'

'I don't know. We were talking . . . The lights went out suddenly . . . ' Sir Richard took out his handkerchief and wiped his streaming forehead. 'It all happened so quickly.' He stopped as Sonia's voice came to them from the hall.

'Are you in there, Father?' she called. 'Is anything wrong?'

Sir Richard made a quick gesture to Kent. 'For God's sake, stop her!' he muttered in a low tone. 'Don't let her come in!' But he was too late, for before Kent could reach the door, Sonia had entered.

She gave one quick glance at the scene before her and stopped dead, the blood draining slowly from her face. 'What — ' she began, but Sir Richard interrupted her.

'It's nothing, child, nothing,' he said hurriedly. 'An accident. Kent, can't you take her away?'

The secretary moved towards her, but Sonia waved him away. 'No, no,' she said unsteadily. 'I'd rather stay. I want to know what's happened.'

A voice from behind her made her start. 'I say, what's all the bother about?' Reginald Stimpson, his face and hair streaming with water and his thin figure wrapped in a bath robe, had appeared in the open doorway. 'I heard a fearful shindy going on; simply couldn't attend to the jolly old ablutions.' He peered over Sonia's shoulder and gave a gasp as he saw the body. 'By jove, I say, what — what's happened?' he stammered.

'Fleming's been shot,' said the chief commissioner grimly.

'Shot!' Sonia's voice was so unlike her own that they thought for a moment a stranger had spoken. 'Oh God, I knew something dreadful was going to happen!'

Sir Richard rose to his feet and, going over to her, took her gently by the arm. 'It's much better you shouldn't stop here, my dear,' he said soothingly. 'I'll take you to Mrs. Bascombe.'

He led her gently from the library, and in the hall they met the talkative Alicia just hurrying down the stairs. Cutting short her stream of questions, the chief commissioner handed Sonia over to her charge, and returned to the room of death.

Stimpson was gazing down in horror at

the thing on the floor, and he looked round as Sir Richard advanced. 'This is terrible, old chappie,' he murmured. 'Who shot him?'

'The Shadow,' answered Sir Richard, and the other drew his dressing-gown closer round him and shivered.

'The Shadow?' he repeated in consternation. 'Why, is he here?'

The chief commissioner nodded slowly. 'According to Fleming, he's somewhere in the house,' he replied. 'If that's so, he won't get away easily. There are detectives watching all the exits.' He turned to Kent. 'Go and see if you can find Detective-Inspector Carr,' he ordered, 'and ask him to come in here. He's outside somewhere, and I don't suppose he knows what's happened yet.' The secretary nodded briefly and hurried away.

'Somewhere in the house!' muttered Stimpson. 'By jove, what a perfectly dreadful thought!' He shivered again and went to the door. 'I think I'll go and dress, old boy,' he remarked. 'I feel rather out of the picture, as it were, in this. If you want any help you can count on me.'

114

He ambled away, and Sir Richard was left alone with all that remained of Chief Inspector Fleming.

He seated himself in a chair, one hand tapping a soft tattoo on the arm, his brows wrinkled in a concentrated effort of thought. The whole thing was impossible, and yet it had happened. Here, in his own house, one of his best men had been murdered before his very eyes, and the murderer had succeeded in getting away. Of course he must be still somewhere in the house, but who was he?

His eyes wandered to the silent figure on the floor. If only Fleming had had time to speak the word — the name that had been hovering on the tip of his tongue when the bullet had crashed through his brain. Just one word that would have solved the mystery. Sir Richard sighed, and looked up as Detective-Inspector Carr, youthful and alert, stepped briskly into the room.

'Your secretary has told me briefly what happened, sir,' he said crisply. 'It's a bad business.'

'It's a terrible affair, Carr,' said Sir

Richard, shaking his head. 'Did Fleming say anything to you regarding the identity of the Shadow?'

'Not a word,' answered Carr. 'He was so occupied with his own thoughts that he scarcely spoke to us at all on the way down.' His grey eyes travelled quickly round the library. 'I suppose you saw nothing that could tell us who fired the shot?'

'No, unfortunately,' answered the chief commissioner. 'The whole thing happened so suddenly that I was taken completely unawares. It was so totally unexpected.'

'Yes, of course.' Carr's gaze rested for a moment on the body. 'Where did the shot come from?'

'From that door,' said Sir Richard, pointing. 'And almost immediately afterwards I felt someone brush past me in the dark.'

The young inspector walked over to the door, opened it, and peered out. 'Where does this passage lead to?' he asked.

'One end leads round to the hall,' explained Sir Richard, 'and there's a door at the other end that opens onto the grounds. But it's made of oak and bolted and barred. No one could have got in or out that way.'

Carr closed the door, thought for a moment, and then came back to the middle of the room. 'I've got a man at the back and front,' he said, 'so no one could possibly have got out after the shot was fired, therefore the murderer must be still in the house. I think I'll start by making a search, sir.'

'We'd better get poor Fleming moved first,' said Sir Richard. 'We'll have to forego the usual routine, since it's impossible to get hold of a doctor in this fog, and we can't leave him lying here till the morning. There's a settee in my study.'

Carr nodded and, stooping over the body, swiftly ran through the pockets. Apart from the usual collection that a man generally carries about with him was a small white box. The inspector opened it.

'What's this, sir?' he asked, holding it out, and the chief commissioner saw that it contained a little gold and platinum charm.

'That's the clue that put Fleming on the trail of the Shadow,' he said soberly, and then as Carr still looked rather puzzled, he briefly explained.

'I see,' said the young inspector when he had finished. 'I think since it's the only clue we've got, you'd better take charge of it for the time being, sir.'

Sir Richard nodded and, crossing over to a safe let into the wall, unlocked it and placed the white box inside, then shut and relocked the door. 'It'll be all right there,' he remarked. 'Now we'd better see about moving this poor fellow.'

They carried the body into Sir Richard's cosy study and laid it on the divan. Then, without further loss of time, they began a swift but systematic search of the house. Starting with the cellars, they worked their way up to the attics, without leaving a square inch of space unexplored. But there was no sign of any intruder. If there was a stranger in Green Lanes, he possessed the power of making himself invisible.

The servants were congregated in the kitchen under Willit's charge, and the rest of the household had been marshalled in the drawing-room by Sir Richard's orders before the search commenced.

'There is certainly no one in the house who can't be accounted for, sir,' said Inspector Carr when they got back to the hall. 'And according to Davis and Larch, no one has attempted to leave.' He looked at the chief commissioner with a puzzled frown.

He would not have been so puzzled had he taken the precaution of searching the roof, for crouching in the shadow of a stack of chimneys, and shivering with cold, was the man whom Willit had let in earlier that evening. And in his heart was a great dread, a dread that had been inspired by the sound of Detective-Inspector Carr's voice when he searched the attic beneath.

9

The Man in the Passage

After a short conference with the chief
commissioner and a word with the two
plainclothes men who were guarding
the exits, Carr made his way back to the
library. Opening the door softly, he
stopped dead on the threshold and
stared at the sight that met his gaze. He
had expected to find the room empty,
instead of which a thin, weedy young
man, immaculately clad in a dinner suit,
was crawling about on his hands and
knees clutching a tape measure and
muttering to himself occasionally under
his breath. So engrossed was he in his
task that he did not hear the door open
or the entrance of the new arrival, and
Carr stood and watched him, a faint
smile curling the corners of his mobile
mouth.

Utterly oblivious to the fact that he had

an audience, Reginald Stimpson continued to measure invisible marks on the carpet, keeping up a running commentary all the while.

At last the young inspector advanced noiselessly to within a yard of the energetic author. 'What the hell *are* you doing?' he remarked loudly.

The startled Mr. Stimpson looked up and scrambled hastily to his feet. 'By jove!' he said breathlessly. 'I never heard you come in, you know, what!'

Carr surveyed the immaculate figure with the vacuous face, and his smile broadened. 'Lost anything?' he enquired pleasantly.

'Er — no.' Stimpson shook his head. 'Whatever put that idea into your head, old chappie?'

'Don't call me old chappie,' snapped the inspector. 'What were you doing there crawling about?'

'Just having a look round, er, old — er, old bean,' said the other rather vaguely.

'Don't call me old bean either.' Carr succeeded in screwing his face into a particularly ferocious expression. 'My name's Carr — Inspector Carr.'

'Awfully sorry,' Stimpson hastened to apologise. 'Fearfully apologetic and all that, er, old thing, what!'

'If you haven't lost anything and you're not looking for anything,' said Carr sternly, 'what *are* you doing?'

'Trying to help, old, er, Inspector,' said the would-be author. 'Got it that time, what?' he added triumphantly. 'Looking for jolly old clues. The place must be simply bristling with 'em, you know.'

'If it is, I ought to see an eye doctor,' said Carr shortly.

'Perhaps you've overlooked them,' began Stimpson innocently.

'What?' roared the inspector, and the other jumped.

'Quite all right, old chappie — er, sorry, I mean Inspector,' he said soothingly, realising that he had made a faux pas. 'I mean, you may have missed some of the little details — no offence, you know — er, quite accidentally, of course! Thought possibly I might bump up against something.'

'You will if you're not careful,'

muttered Carr grimly. 'Something mighty hard!'

'I rather fancy myself as a detective, you know,' Stimpson went on confidentially. 'Sort of got the instinct. You've got it, too, of course. In fact, we've both got it badly! I write stories, you know — thrillers. Now there's always something at the scene of the crime — a bit of mud or a cigarette end or some little trifle like that, that gives the criminal chappie away at once. Didn't you find anything like that, old — '

'Carr!' shouted the exasperated inspector, and Stimpson blinked and dropped his eyeglass.

'Fearfully sorry, old boy,' he said hastily, and stuck the monocle back in his eye. 'As I was saying — this Shadow chappie must have left some clue, you know. It stands to reason. You can't go round shooting people without leaving clues! It positively isn't done, old thing!' He shook his head emphatically.

'Now listen to me, Mr — ' began Carr impressively, but Stimpson, having once got going on his favourite topic, was not to be put off easily.

'Stimpson, old boy — Reginald Stimpson, that's my name,' he broke in, beaming good-humouredly at the other. 'Talking about clues — '

'I'm not talking about clues,' snapped the inspector loudly.

Reggie appeared surprised, and a trifle pained. 'Oh, but you must, you know,' he protested. 'You've positively got to! If we're going to work together on this jolly old business, we simply *must* talk about clues.'

Carr drew a deep breath of exasperation; a little of Mr. Stimpson went a long way with most people. 'We are *not* going to work together,' he explained clearly and carefully. 'If I want any help I'll get it from Scotland Yard. I don't want any amateurs running round.'

'But you don't quite understand — '

'If it amuses you to go about measuring things with — that,' continued the inspector, pointing at the dangling tape measure, 'carry on! I don't want to spoil anyone's enjoyment. But don't do it here. Go and — and measure the bathroom!'

124

'The — the bathroom?' repeated Stimpson stupidly.

'Yes — or anywhere else you like,' grunted Carr, 'so long as it's far enough away from *this* room.'

'I say, you know,' exclaimed the other as though the fact had suddenly dawned on him, 'I don't believe you jolly well *want* me to help you.'

Carr looked at him and nodded slowly. 'You've the makings of a detective in you after all,' he said sarcastically. 'I couldn't have worked things out better myself!'

Stimpson stared at him for a moment in silence and then shrugged his shoulders. 'Oh, very well,' he said resignedly, walking to the door. 'You'll be frightfully sorry about this, old chappie, frightfully sorry! However, it's your loss.' He turned with his hand on the knob. 'When I've caught the Shadow all by myself you'll feel horribly peeved — horribly peeved! Oh, you'll be so cross!' He went out, slamming the door behind him, and Carr's face relaxed into a broad grin.

It was only for a moment, however. The next, his brows had drawn together in a frown. This case was his big chance, and so far he could not see even a glimmer of light. The Shadow had killed and vanished, but where had he vanished to? He could not have left the house, and he certainly was not in it now — unless *he was one of the people who were known to be there*!

The idea was a startling one, but it offered the only solution, and was made the more credible by the fact that Fleming had obviously come to Green Lanes with the expectation of finding the Shadow already there. But who among the household could possibly be the unknown criminal? The only strangers present at the time of Fleming's death were the Silvertons.

Carr made a mental note to investigate them more thoroughly. Yet it seemed absurd. He was faced with the ridiculous proposition that the Shadow had knowingly and willingly walked into the lion's den. It was almost as unbelievable as a burglar trying to break into Scotland Yard. And yet, the facts . . .

His thoughts snapped off short as from

outside, close at hand, came a shrill scream laden with fear and terror!

He swung round and raced to the door, his heart pounding. As he wrenched it open, Sonia, her face ashen and her eyes wide and terrified, almost fell into his arms.

'Miss Lane!' he cried anxiously. 'What's the matter?'

She clung to him for a second, speechless, her breath coming in quick, sobbing gasps. 'There's a man — a man in the passage!' she managed to force the words through her quivering lips.

'Sunny!' Sir Richard's voice came anxiously from the hall. 'What is it, child? What made you scream?'

He appeared at the door, his face tense with alarm. Sonia pulled herself together with a tremendous effort.

'I — ' She pushed the hair back from her forehead with a shaking hand. 'There was a man — at the foot of the stairs. I touched his face in the dark. It was horrible!' She shuddered and stifled a sob.

'I'll go and see.' Carr hurried out and

Sir Richard led his trembling daughter over to a chair.

'Come, come,' he said tenderly, seating himself beside her on the arm and patting her hand. 'Your nerves are overstrained, dear, and I'm not surprised. Perhaps it was only one of the servants.'

She shook her head quickly. 'It wasn't,' she said. 'I know it wasn't. He had a bearded chin and he was crouching against the banisters.'

Beverley Kent came in with a white face. 'Who was that screaming?' he asked sharply; and, catching sight of Sonia, 'Miss Lane! Are you hurt?'

She forced a wintery smile. 'No, I'm all right, thank you. I was frightened for a moment, that's all.'

'Did you see anyone in the hall, Kent?' asked the chief commissioner.

'Anyone in the hall?' The secretary shook his head. 'No — only Willit.'

'Sonia says there was a man crouching at the foot of the stairs,' explained Sir Richard.

'There was nobody there when I came down,' declared Kent. 'I was up in my

128

room when I heard the scream.'

The chief commissioner looked perplexed. 'Are you *sure* you didn't imagine it, Sunny?' he said.

'Positive,' she replied decisively. 'I was coming downstairs, and when I reached the bottom I put out my hand to steady myself. It was dark because the hall light was out — '

'*Out?*' broke in Kent excitedly. 'It was *on* when I came down just now.'

She looked startled. 'Well, it wasn't on *then*,' she said emphatically. 'My hand, instead of touching the banister as I expected, struck against something soft and yielding — a man's face.' She shivered at the recollection.

'What was he like?' asked the chief commissioner.

'I don't know. I just caught sight of a crouching figure and then I — ran.' She had almost recovered from the shock and was rapidly gaining something of her usual composure.

'It's curious about that light being out,' remarked Kent thoughtfully, and Sir Richard nodded.

'You said Willit was in the hall. Perhaps he put it out,' he suggested. 'Let's ask him.' He went over and pressed the bell.

'You remember the man Alicia said she saw looking in the window this afternoon?' said Sonia.

'Or imagined she saw,' answered Sir Richard.

'No, I believe she really did see someone,' Sonia went on, shaking her head. 'She said he had a rough, unshaven face — do you think it could have been the same man?'

The chief commissioner rubbed his chin. 'How could he have got in?' he said doubtfully.

'*Somebody's* got in,' declared Sonia. 'The face I touched in the dark belonged to no one we know in this house.'

There came a soft tap on the door and Willit entered. 'You rang, sir?' he said respectfully.

'Did you put the hall light out just now?' asked Sir Richard without preliminary.

'I, sir? No, sir,' answered the butler. He

looked from one to the other in slight surprise.

'You haven't touched it at all?'

'Not since I put it on just before tea, sir.'

'All right, Willit.' The chief commissioner nodded a dismissal and the butler bowed and withdrew. 'It wasn't Willit, you see,' he said thoughtfully.

'*Someone* put the light out.' Sonia's voice was scarcely above a whisper. 'Someone who didn't want to be seen going up the stairs.'

There was a constrained silence while each was occupied with the startling thought that Sonia's adventure had given rise to.

Someone was in the house whom they didn't know — had never seen: a killer lurking about the dark corridors. And the knowledge was anything but reassuring!

10

What Sonia Knew

It was Beverley Kent who first broke that long silence. 'Where's that chap Silverton?' he asked suddenly. 'I suppose it couldn't have been him?'

Sonia shook her head impatiently. 'No, no, I tell you the man had a beard,' she answered a little irritably. 'Besides, I left Mr. Silverton a few minutes before in the drawing room with his sister.'

'Anyway, he wouldn't have had any reason to put the light out,' remarked the chief commissioner.

'No, I suppose not.' The secretary gently stroked his small moustache and frowned thoughtfully. 'It seems curious, though,' he said. 'We don't know anything about him, and he arrived here just before Fleming.' He looked at Sir Richard, and the latter started.

'Are you suggesting — ' he began.

'That he's the Shadow?' broke in Kent. 'Well, why not, sir? You can't get away from facts.' He paused. 'Fleming came down here expecting to find the Shadow,' he went on after a moment. 'He brought Carr and two other men with him. He knew who the Shadow was, and he expected to find him here. The only stranger who was here when Fleming arrived was Silverton. It strikes me as a curious coincidence.'

'It *is* a curious coincidence, but it can't be anything else,' exclaimed the chief commissioner. 'Fleming can't possibly have known that Silverton's car was going to break down outside the house.'

Kent pursed his lips and pulled gently at the lobe of his right ear. 'No,' he answered slowly, 'he can't have known that, but . . . ' He left the sentence unfinished.

'But what?' asked Sonia eagerly. She had been listening with the closest attention.

'But the car breaking down may have been a put-up job,' concluded the secretary, emphasising each word.

Sir Richard made an impatient gesture. 'But why?' he argued. 'Just let us suppose for a moment that this man, Silverton, is the Shadow — why should he come here, of all places, and how could Fleming have known that he was coming?'

Beverley Kent shrugged his shoulders. 'Only Fleming could have answered that, sir,' he replied. 'Pity he was so close about the matter.'

'A great pity,' agreed the commissioner. 'But he was always like that. Hated to say anything to anyone until he'd got all his evidence cut and dried. We used to call him Bombshell Fleming at the Yard, because of his fondness for springing surprises.'

'That charm you were talking about this afternoon,' said Sonia suddenly. 'What happened to it?'

Sir Richard looked down at her in surprise. 'Fleming brought it with him; it's in there,' he said, jerking his head towards the wall in which the safe was set.

'Can I see it?' she asked in a low voice.

The expression of surprise on his face

deepened as she put the question to him. 'What for, child?'

'Just curiosity,' she said evasively. 'But I should like to see it.'

'I don't think — ' he began, but she interrupted him.

'Please,' she coaxed, and the old man, who had never willingly refused her anything in her life, gave way.

'I suppose there's no reason why you shouldn't,' he remarked, 'though I really can't understand why you want to.'

He walked over to the safe, feeling in his pockets. Halfway across the room, he stopped with a sudden exclamation. 'Confound it!' he muttered. 'What did I do with them?'

'What's the matter, sir?' asked Kent quickly.

'I haven't got the keys,' said Sir Richard with a trace of annoyance. 'Must have left them upstairs. Careless of me.'

'I'll get them for you, sir,' offered the secretary, moving towards the door, but his employer stopped him.

'No, no, I'll go,' he replied hastily, and went out.

Beverley Kent lit a cigarette after he had gone and stood silently looking into the fire, every now and again darting little sidelong glances at Sonia, who was sitting with her chin cupped in her hands, deep in thought. From the expression on her face, her thoughts were not pleasant ones, for a frown wrinkled the usually smooth expanse of her brow, and her eyes were troubled.

'Why are you so anxious to see that charm, Miss Lane?' said Kent suddenly.

She started at the sound of his voice and looked up. 'Merely curiosity,' she replied lightly.

He shook his head with a little smile. 'That's not the real reason,' he answered. 'There's something else. I knew that when you were asking Sir Richard to show it to you.'

Her mouth tightened and she looked annoyed. 'Really, Mr. Kent,' she said, 'are you politely calling me a liar?'

He laughed good-humouredly. 'It did sound like that, didn't it?' he admitted. 'But that wasn't what I meant.' And then suddenly becoming serious, he added,

'You're worried about something. What is it?'

She was silent, but her eyes dropped, and after waiting a few minutes he went on: 'I don't want to pry into your secrets, of course, but there's just a possibility that I could help you. If you think I could, please tell me what it is that's troubling you.'

She continued to remain silent, and Kent was beginning to believe that he had really offended her, when she beckoned him to come nearer. 'Sit there,' she said, speaking in a whisper and glancing swiftly round the room.

He sat down on the settee by her side, and she leaned towards him. 'If I tell you something, will you give me your word that you won't repeat it to anyone?' Her face was pale and strained, the earnestness in her voice unmistakable. Wondering what she was about to tell him, Kent nodded.

'I give you my word,' he answered briefly.

'Not even to Father?' she persisted.

'I promise you I won't breathe a

syllable to anybody,' he declared, secretly amused at her vehemence.

'Well, then . . . ' She paused, and her voice dropped until it was scarcely audible. 'That charm in the safe . . . I believe I've seen it before.'

'What?' If she had intended to startle him, she had most certainly succeeded.

'Father described it this afternoon,' she went on hurriedly. 'I'm sure I've seen it before.'

He sprang up, his face incredulous. 'Good God! Where?' he asked, his voice husky with excitement.

'Here, in this house,' she replied.

'Miss Lane, do you know what you're saying?' He looked down at her, his face grave.

She nodded. 'Yes. That charm belonged to the Shadow, and if I'm right — ' She broke off and, rising abruptly to her feet, went over to the fireplace and rested her elbows on the mantelpiece. 'Oh, I can't be right,' she muttered almost to herself. 'It's too dreadful!'

'What do you mean?' he asked.

'I can't tell you any more,' she replied,

shaking her head. 'I ought not to have told you anything. If I'm wrong, I should be doing the person I suspect irreparable harm.'

'But whom do you suspect?' he persisted.

'I can't tell you,' she repeated. 'I can't tell anyone yet. I'm not sure.'

Was it the draught that had caused the door leading into the passage to swing open an inch? Whatever it was, they were too occupied to notice it.

'You ought to tell Sir Richard,' said the secretary, pacing restlessly up and down.

'But I may be entirely wrong,' she answered. 'Think how dreadful it would be if I were.'

He stopped and looked at her steadily. 'Miss Lane,' he said very seriously, 'don't you realise that you are withholding evidence that might lead to the arrest of this murderer, and that it's obviously my duty to acquaint Sir Richard with what you have just told me?'

Her eyes filled with sudden panic. 'No, no, you mustn't do that!' she cried. 'You promised!'

'I know,' he answered, 'and I shall keep that promise. Will you be certain when you've seen that charm?'

'Yes, quite,' she answered.

'Then will you promise, in your turn,' he continued, 'that as soon as you have seen it, you will tell Sir Richard everything you suspect?'

She nodded without hesitation, and had opened her lips to reply when Mrs. Bascombe came tripping into the room.

'Oh, there you are, Sonia darling!' she exclaimed, fluttering over to the fireplace. 'I've been wondering what could have become of you.' She looked archly from Kent to Sonia. 'I do hope I'm not intruding,' she added with a little giggle, and immediately settled herself comfortably in a chair. 'Did I hear someone scream a little while ago? I thought I did, but you can't hear very well in the drawing-room with the door shut, and Miss Silverton said she didn't hear anything. I wanted to come and see, but she seemed frightened at being left alone.'

Beverley Kent raised his head sharply. 'Wasn't her brother with her, Mrs.

Bascombe?' he asked.

That lady shook her red head daintily. 'No, he left us directly after Sonia,' she replied. '*Such* a charming man, and *so* interesting to talk to. I feel quite ashamed for ever having thought he could be a burglar!'

'Good gracious!' Sonia gave a little laugh. 'When did you imagine Mr. Silverton was a burglar?'

Mrs. Bascombe cocked her head to one side like a knowing parrot. 'Well, you see, darling,' she explained, 'it seemed so extraordinary, the car breaking down and all that. One reads of such dreadful things in the papers, and after the terrible way that poor policeman was killed . . . ' She made a little clucking sound with her teeth. 'Of course, directly I saw him, I knew at once that he was quite all right. I'm sure he shaves at least twice a day.'

'What on earth has that got to do with it?' asked the secretary in amazement.

'He couldn't possibly be a burglar and shave,' answered Mrs. Bascombe with conviction. 'They've always got rough, stubbly chins. Besides, he told me he was a broker, though I don't think he looks the least like one. A friend of mine once had the brokers in, and they weren't the least like Mr. Silverton.'

Kent suppressed a chuckle. 'I'm afraid you're a trifle mixed up,' he said. 'There's a lot of difference between brokers' men and brokers, though one often leads to the other.'

Sonia, who had been fidgeting uneasily, turned towards him impatiently. 'Father's taking a long time, isn't he?' she said. 'I wish you'd go and find him. Something may have happened.'

Kent looked a trifle sceptical. 'Like what?' he asked.

'I don't know.' She twisted her hands together nervously. 'But please, do go and see if he's all right.'

'Right you are, I'll go,' he said, crossing over to the door.

'I understand exactly how you feel, darling,' said Mrs. Bascombe complacently when they were alone. 'I'm just the same. My nerves are in a shocking state. I must say that I'm most disappointed in the police; they're not at all what I expected. I used to think they were so romantic, too. I was talking to this man, what's-his-name, Carr, just now; and do you know, he hasn't found a single mysterious footprint, and he hasn't got a microscope or even a magnifying glass!'

Sonia smiled. 'Detectives only do that sort of thing in novels,' she said.

Mrs. Bascombe nodded wisely. 'But they always succeed in catching the criminal, dear,' she retorted. 'You must admit that. I've never read any book yet in which they've failed!'

Before Sonia had time to offer a reply to this amazing argument, the sound of a shot echoed loudly from somewhere in the house. It was followed instantly by two others fired in rapid succession, and then a hoarse cry of pain!

11

The Missing Keys

Mrs. Bascombe collapsed in her chair with a shrill scream of fear as Sonia sprang to her feet, her face the colour of chalk. At the same moment, Carr's voice came faintly from outside, shouting: 'Davis! Search that staircase! He's above, man, on the second landing!'

Hurried footsteps stumbled towards the library door. It was flung open and the young inspector staggered in, followed by Sir Richard. Sonia caught her breath with a gasp of alarm at the sight of him, for Carr's face was deathly pale, and the blood was pouring from a long gash in the side of his forehead.

'Carr, are you badly hurt?' Sir Richard asked anxiously as he bent over the young detective, who had sunk into a chair and was dabbing at his head with a handkerchief.

'No, sir,' he answered in a voice that was a little shaky. 'It's only a scratch. One of the bullets grazed the side of my head. I'll be all right in a minute. The devil! He nearly got me.'

'Who was it?' asked the chief commissioner.

'God knows, sir,' said Carr. 'It took me completely by surprise. Davis and I had just finished combing the house for the man Miss Lane saw on the stairs; there wasn't a trace of him, and we were returning to the hall when someone opened fire from above.'

'I was on the first landing,' said Sir Richard, 'and I saw no one.'

'Then he must have been higher up, sir,' declared the inspector. 'Somewhere in this house there's a killer loose. It may be someone we've never seen, or it may be someone we know. But I'm going to get him, and to start with I want to know where everybody was, and what they were doing at the time those shots were fired.'

'I say, this is getting awfully thrilling, what?' drawled a voice. 'The bally shooting season's started!' Mr. Stimpson strolled into the room, his face twisted into his usual inane smile.

Carr looked at him grimly. 'Where have you been?' he asked curtly.

The other adjusted his monocle carefully before replying. 'Looking for clues, old boy,' he said cheerfully.

'Where?' snapped the inspector.

'Oh, all over the place,' answered Mr. Stimpson airily. 'Upstairs, downstairs, but not in my lady's chamber.' He chuckled. 'Women don't like it, old boy.'

'Were you upstairs just now?' said Carr sharply.

'While the shooting was going on?' enquired Reggie, and he shook his head. 'No bally fear, old thing!'

'Where were you?'

'In the dining room, old boy.' He strolled over and perched himself on the edge of the writing table. 'Having a drink.'

Carr surveyed the thin figure, and his eyes narrowed. 'Anybody with you?' he asked.

Mr. Stimpson shook his head again. 'Not a soul,' he declared. 'I was all on my little lonesome, but don't get it into your head that I'm a secret drinker or anything like that,' he added hastily.

'Then I've only your word that you were there at all?' said Carr.

'Oh, no, old top.' The other slipped from his position on the table and sauntered across to the young inspector. 'Johnny Walker, old boy.' He thrust his face close to Carr's and breathed gently. 'No getting away from that, what? Eighteen-sixty and still going strong!'

The detective pushed him away with a gesture of annoyance and turned to the chief commissioner. 'Now, sir,' he said crisply, 'what about you?'

Sir Richard looked a little annoyed. 'Me?' he replied, frowning. 'Surely you — '

'I'm sorry, sir,' said Carr firmly but respectfully, 'but I can't leave anyone out. You were on the first landing, you say?'

Sir Richard considered. 'No,' he answered, 'I was in my bedroom when the firing actually started. I came out at once.'

'Did you see where the shots came from?'

'No, I couldn't say. By the time I

reached the end of the passage it was all over.'

'What were you doing in your room, sir?' asked Carr, and added, 'I'm sorry to question you like this, but — '

'That's all right, I quite understand,' Sir Richard waved aside his apologies. 'I was looking for the keys of the safe, but they've disappeared.'

'Disappeared?' It was Sonia who spoke, and her voice was shrill and startled.

'Yes, it's most extraordinary.' The chief commissioner scratched his chin irritably. 'I've searched everywhere, but they've gone.'

'Does that mean you can't open the safe?' asked his daughter quickly.

He nodded. 'I'm afraid it does, my dear.'

A curious expression crept into Carr's eyes for a moment as he looked across at his chief. 'Do you think it possible that the keys have been stolen?' he asked quietly.

'They must have been,' declared Sir Richard. 'I've searched my room thoroughly and they're not there.'

'Perhaps you left them somewhere else,' suggested Mrs. Bascombe brightly. 'Poor dear George was always most trying with keys. I remember once — '

Sir Richard, who at that moment was not in the least interested in what she remembered, hastily broke in. 'No, no, I distinctly recollect leaving them on my dressing table when I went up to get a handkerchief.'

Carr pursed his lips thoughtfully. 'The door of your room, I suppose, was unlocked, sir?' he enquired. 'Anyone could have gone in?'

The chief commissioner nodded, and after a moment's pause the young inspector swung round and faced Sonia and Mrs. Bascombe. 'You two ladies were in here, weren't you?' he asked abruptly, and they replied in the affirmative. 'Then that leaves the other lady — what's-her-name, Miss Silverton; her brother; your secretary, Sir Richard; and the servants to be accounted for,' he continued. 'I should like to speak to them.'

'Mr. Kent was in here with us,' said Sonia. 'I asked him to go and find out why you were taking so long. Didn't you see him?'

'No, I haven't seen a sign of him,' answered Sir Richard.

'That's strange,' said Carr sharply. 'When did he go, Miss Lane?'

'A few minutes before the shots,' she replied.

A puzzled expression crossed the inspector's face. 'Where the deuce can he be?' he muttered. 'He must have heard the firing. So must Silverton and his sister. It's funny that none of them have turned up to see what the row was about.'

Mrs. Bascombe uttered a little shrill cry. 'Perhaps they've all been murdered!' she wailed.

'Nonsense!' snapped the chief commissioner. 'Probably they're helping Davis to search the house.'

'Probably,' agreed Carr, but his voice lacked conviction. 'Will you ring for your butler, sir?'

Sir Richard signed to Sonia, who was nearest the bell, and she obeyed. Her finger was on the push when the door was flung violently open, and a big, broad-shouldered man burst unceremoniously into the room.

'What is it, Davis?' rapped Carr as his subordinate paused, breathing heavily.

'It's Mr. Kent, sir,' panted the sergeant. 'I've just found him unconscious in his room, and he seems to have had a nasty crack on the back of his head!'

12

The Open Window

They received the news in stunned silence, and the expressions on their faces in any other circumstances would have been amusing.

'Good God!' breathed Sir Richard at last. 'What's going to happen next?'

Mr. Stimpson, who had strolled over to the window and had apparently been taking not the slightest interest in the proceedings, suddenly showed signs of life. 'By jove, poor old Kent,' he drawled. 'Now isn't that remarkable!'

'Why is it remarkable?' The question came from Carr like a lightning flash.

Mr. Stimpson surveyed him innocently. 'I don't really know, old boy,' he said with a bland smile. 'Just thought so, that's all.'

The inspector's lips compressed into a thin line, but he checked the angry retort that he had been on the verge of making, and turned to Davis. 'Is Mr. Kent badly hurt?' he asked.

'No, sir,' the man said, shaking his head. 'Just stunned, that's all. He was recovering when I found him.'

'You'd better go back to him,' ordered Carr, 'and stop there until I come. I suppose you didn't find any trace of the shooter?'

'Only the spent cartridge shells.' Davis advanced and held out three little gleaming brass objects. 'On the second landing; he used an automatic.'

Carr took them, looked at them, and slipped them into his pocket. 'We shall probably find that the bullet that killed Fleming was fired from an automatic,' he said. 'Where's Larch?'

'Guarding the back exit,' said the sergeant, and added: 'Inspector Wallace, of the local police, has just arrived, sir. Chief Inspector Fleming left a message for him at the police station, but it took him a long time to make his way up here in the fog. He's watching the front.'

'Good,' Carr said, nodding quickly. 'Tell 'em to stop where they are; they're to let no one either in or out, do you understand? No one.' The plainclothes man nodded. 'Now go back to Mr. Kent.'

Davis withdrew, and the chief commissioner looked across at Carr. 'This is terrible!' he muttered. 'Terrible! We must do something to find this man. Nobody's safe while he remains unknown.'

'I'm going to find him, sir,' answered Carr grimly. 'The trouble is, we've got so little to go on. We don't know whether he's a stranger or one of ourselves. For all I know, he might be *you*.' If he saw the sudden start that Sonia gave, he made no comment, but went on: 'And for all you know, he might be *me*, or Mr. Stimpson, or Willit, or Mr. Silverton.'

'Or Mr. Kent,' suggested Stimpson casually.

'Yes, or Mr. Kent. Except in that case, he would appear to have hit himself on the head,' agreed Carr.

'Oh, quite. I'd forgotten that, old boy.' Reggie turned away, a little crestfallen.

'On the other hand, he may be a complete stranger,' continued the inspector, 'whom none of us have yet seen.'

There came a subdued tap on the door, and Willit entered hesitantly. His face was pale and his hands trembled visibly, though he made a desperate effort to appear calm.

Carr eyed him keenly. 'Willit,' he said, 'where were all the servants when that shooting was going on?'

'In the kitchen, sir.' The butler's voice was a little unsteady.

'Where were you?'

'Me, sir?' Willit appeared momentarily confused. 'In — in my room, sir.'

'Where's that?'

'At the top of the house, sir.' The old man's lips seemed dry, for he passed his tongue over them before continuing. 'I heard the noise and came down.'

'I never saw you.'

'No, sir. Sergeant Davis was coming up the stairs, and I waited to let him pass me.'

'Did he see you?'

'Yes, sir.' Willit was evidently gaining confidence, for his voice was stronger and more distinct. 'He asked me if I'd seen anyone upstairs.'

'Had you seen anyone?'

'No, sir.' The answer came quickly and firmly.

Carr paused, his eyes fixed steadily on the old man, and then suddenly and sharply he leaned forward. 'Willit, let me see your hand.'

The butler stiffened, and then slowly he extended his left hand.

'No, not that one,' said Carr sternly. 'The *right* hand, Willit.'

He waited while the butler, his face grey, dropped his left hand and reluctantly raised his right. Then Carr took a step forward. 'Ever fired an automatic pistol?' he asked softly.

'An — an automatic pistol, sir?' repeated Willit stupidly.

'Yes.' The tone of Carr's voice was almost conversational. 'When an automatic is fired, the blowback leaves a slight burn between the thumb and forefinger of the pistol hand.'

'Is — is that so, sir?' whispered the butler huskily. 'I've . . . never fired one, sir.'

'Then how did you get that mark?' The

question came like a bullet from a gun, and the inspector pointed at the butler's extended right hand.

Willit dropped his hand quickly, but not before they had all seen the reddish scar between the forefinger and thumb. 'I — I burnt my hand this afternoon, sir,' he said in confusion. 'On the kitchen stove.'

Carr went over to the old man and, seizing his hand, raised it to his nostrils and sniffed. 'There's no smell of cordite,' he remarked. 'But that doesn't prove anything. You may have washed your hands since.'

'What do you mean, sir?' exclaimed the butler indignantly. 'Surely you're not accusing me of — '

'I'm not accusing anybody,' snapped the inspector. 'I'm just trying to find out.' He took a restless turn up and down the room, and stopped opposite Willit again. 'Find Miss Silverton and her brother and ask them to come in here,' he said, and the butler bowed and withdrew.

'It's absurd to suspect Willit, Carr,' said Sir Richard. 'He's been with me for years.'

'He may have been, sir,' retorted the inspector, 'but I'm suspecting everybody until I've proved that they can't be the Shadow. It's the only way. I'm rather interested to know why this man Silverton hasn't showed up. He must have heard the shots unless he's stone deaf, and you'd think natural curiosity would have brought him along to see what all the racket's about.'

'He may have been hit on the jolly old dome-piece, too,' interjected Stimpson brightly.

'Oh, Mr. Stimpson,' said Mrs. Bascombe with a shudder, 'how can you talk so flippantly? We may all be murdered before morning!'

'Sorry,' apologised Reggie. 'I was only making a suggestion. Perhaps he's gone to bed.'

'Why should he go to bed?' snapped Carr irritably.

The other grinned. 'To snooze, old boy,' he replied blandly. 'To close the giddy optic. In other words, to sleep, old bean — sorry, it slipped out.'

'I wish you'd follow its example!'

growled the exasperated detective.

Mr. Stimpson surveyed him with what he intended to be a dignified stare, but which more nearly resembled a sheep in pain. 'All right, I will,' he said stiffly. 'I'll toddle off and find some cigarettes. Under the influence of tobacco, I shall no doubt find a solution to the giddy old mystery. Nothing like smoke to let loose the floodgates of inspiration.' He lounged over to the door. 'You try it, old boy,' he drawled pleasantly. 'All you want is an ounce of shag, a dressing gown, and a violin, and you'll catch the Shadow in no time. There's not a criminal living who can resist the combination.' He wandered out, closing the door behind him, and Carr snorted with disgust.

'Of all the brainless idiots!' he muttered.

The chief commissioner smiled indulgently. 'I'm afraid he's not overburdened with intelligence,' he admitted. 'He's a good fellow, though; do anything for anybody.' He went over to the writing table and helped himself to a cigar. 'I think I'll go up and see how Kent's getting on,' he added, 'and — what is it, Willit?'

The butler had entered hurriedly without the preliminary of knocking. 'It's the window, sir,' he stammered excitedly. 'I thought I'd better tell you. It's open.'

'What's that?' broke in Carr. 'Which window?'

'Downstairs, sir, near the kitchen door,' replied the agitated butler. 'I'll swear it was shut and fastened when I passed it before.'

In two strides the young inspector was at the door. 'Show me!' he snapped, and followed Willit into the hall.

The woman called Moya came out of the drawing room as they passed and, seeing Carr, drew back and waited until he had disappeared down the stairs. There was a glint of fear in her eyes and a cold feeling of despair in her heart, for none knew better than she the meaning of that open window. It was the last desperate resource of a man striving to save himself from the shadow of the gallows, and she hoped with all her soul that he would be successful.

13

A Handkerchief

Sonia moved away from the window through which she had been staring and began to walk aimlessly about the library. Her face was thoughtful, and her eyes gloomy and troubled. The fog showed no signs of dispersing — she had opened the window for a second and stepped out onto the balcony, and if anything, it seemed to have got thicker. There flashed through her mind the weird idea that nature had wrapped the house and its occupants in a shroud.

Her head was filled with a chaotic jumble of thoughts, uppermost among which appeared the vague picture of a golden hand holding in its clenched fingers a sphere of platinum . . . She must have made a mistake. There must be two similar charms. Any other explanation was too horrible, too wildly impossible;

and yet if she were right, she knew the Shadow. Knew also why he had been able to baffle the police for so long, and the reason that had brought Chief Inspector Fleming hurrying post-haste through the fog to Green Lanes when he had discovered the blackmailer's identity. If only she could get a glimpse of the little trinket, she would be certain. It was this suspense that was so terrible — hoping against hope that she was wrong, when all the time her reason kept telling her that she was right.

The disappearance of the key had been a clever move, and it had achieved its object. Nothing short of a skilled safe-breaker could reach that damning piece of evidence now, for Sir Richard's safe was of the latest pattern. Over and over again she considered the advisability of taking Inspector Carr into her confidence; of telling him her doubts and fears. But each time she decided against this course. There still lingered in her mind a final hope, a desperate doubt that she had made a mistake, and she had no wish to precipitate the terrible scandal that would inevitably ensue if she spoke, even though her suspicions were afterward proved to be wrong. The only thing she could do was to wait until she could see the charm, and finally prove to herself one way or the other whether her suspicions were justified.

Mrs. Bascombe, who had been so unusually silent that Sonia had concluded she was asleep, suddenly raised her head. 'You know, darling, I've been thinking,' she announced. 'I shouldn't be at all surprised if that man — what's-his-name? Bar, Tar — '

'Carr,' corrected Sonia.

'That's the man.' Mrs. Bascombe nodded her head several times with extraordinary rapidity. 'Well, I shouldn't be surprised if he didn't know a great deal more than he says.'

'What do you mean, Alicia?' Sonia came over to the fireplace and looked questioningly at her companion.

'I mean that he may be at the bottom of all these terrible happenings,' replied Alicia. 'I'm sure there's something in what I say.'

Sonia stared at her blankly. 'Don't talk nonsense!' she said rather sharply. 'How could he be?'

Mrs. Bascombe nodded her head wisely. 'It's not nonsense,' she affirmed. 'I don't like the man. I think he's most rude and inquisitive, and I noticed something a little while ago that made me very suspicious.'

'What was that?' asked Sonia curiously.

'His chin, darling,' answered Mrs. Bascombe, dropping her voice impressively. 'It was quite stubbly. I'm certain he never shaved this morning.'

Sonia laughed, a rather relieved laugh. For a second she had wondered what the older woman was going to say. 'Really, Alicia,' she protested, 'you're too ridiculous at times.'

An expression of annoyance crossed the other's painted face. 'Well, you'll see,' she said stubbornly. 'It's very seldom I'm mistaken in a man.'

'You must have had a lot of experience,' broke in the husky voice of Moya Silverton with a sneer. Unnoticed by either, she had come into the room softly.

Mrs. Bascombe twisted round in her chair. 'My dear!' she exclaimed. 'Where have you been, and where is your brother?'

Moya came over to the fireplace and warmed her hands. 'I don't know,' she answered. 'I thought he was in here. I've been in the drawing room.'

'Alone?' asked Sonia.

She nodded. 'Yes, I was waiting for Jim to come back.' She shivered slightly. 'I hope nothing has happened to him.'

'I'm sure that no one would harm Mr. Silverton, my dear,' said Mrs. Bascombe soothingly. 'He's such a charming man, and so good-looking, I think.'

'I doubt if the Shadow would take his looks into consideration,' remarked Sonia sarcastically.

Moya glanced up at her, her dark, eager eyes suffused with terror. 'It's all dreadful, isn't it?' she whispered. 'I've never been so frightened in my life.' She spoke truly, but the Shadow was not one of her fears.

There was a long silence; the atmosphere of tragedy and gloom that had descended on the house appeared to have infected even the voluble Mrs. Bascombe. The vague sense of some brooding presence, malignant and active in their midst, was felt by everyone. And it was all the more terrifying because they were unaware from whence the danger emanated.

Sir Richard came in presently, looking tired and worried. 'Poor Kent's had a nasty blow,' he said in answer to Sonia's enquiry. 'He's still a bit dazed, but luckily it's nothing serious. I've just sent Willit up with some coffee. Where's Carr?'

'He hasn't come back yet,' answered Sonia, and the chief commissioner nodded absently.

'I've arranged for rooms for yourself and your brother, Miss Silverton,' he said abruptly, turning to Moya, and she thanked him. 'By the way,' he continued, 'where is he? Have you seen anything of him?' She shook her head. 'It's most extraordinary,' he went on, rubbing his chin. 'I've made enquiries among the servants, and no one seems to have seen him. He must be somewhere in the house. He can't have gone out without being seen. Unless — ' He paused as an idea struck him. 'Unless he went through that window,' he added.

'If he's gone and — ' began Moya, but she was interrupted as the door was flung open and Reginald Stimpson burst eagerly into the room, his face beaming with excitement.

'I say, all of you!' he cried delightedly. 'I told you that the jolly old tobacco would yield results. I've found a clue!'

Sir Richard swung round. 'What?' he exclaimed.

'Yes. Where's dear old Carr?' Stimpson looked round for the inspector, and his face fell. 'Not here? What a pity! Never mind.' He faced the others, his hands in his jacket pockets. 'I went up to my room to get the old cigarette, and thought I'd have a look round, and look what I've found on the second landing.' He pulled a white object out of his pocket and held it up.

'What is it?' demanded the chief commissioner.

'A handkerchief, old boy!' cried the triumphant Mr. Stimpson. 'And it's been used to wipe a pistol; you can see the jolly old powder marks!'

'Whose is it?' asked Sir Richard, eagerly crossing over to his side.

Reggie shook his head. 'Haven't the faintest idea, old thing,' he replied. 'I was so excited I didn't stop to look.' He turned the piece of white linen over in his fingers, peering at it through his monocle. 'By jove!' he cried. 'There are some initials in this corner. Look! R.B.'

Sonia's face went the colour of chalk. 'R.B.?' she repeated huskily. 'Why, Father, it's one of yours!'

'Mine?' exclaimed Sir Richard, and he snatched it from Stimpson's hand. 'Good gracious, so it is!'

'Oh, God, how horrible!' murmured Sonia almost inaudibly.

For the finding of that handkerchief had confirmed her worst fears!

14

The Man Who Got Mud-Stained

'I had to tell someone, Mr. Carr,' said Sonia desperately. 'I couldn't keep it to myself any longer.'

The young inspector looked across at her, his eyes full of sympathy, and nodded.

They were standing in the long oak-panelled dining-room at Green Lanes. After the finding of the handkerchief, Sonia had felt that she must get away to think over this new developments, and was crossing the hall to go to her room when she had met Carr coming from the direction of the kitchen. A sudden impulse had caused her to draw the inspector into the dining-room and pour into his willing and astonished ears all her doubts and fears that had culminated in the discovery of that square of soiled linen.

'I am very glad you *have* told me, Miss Lane,' he said softly. 'I wish you had done so before. Have you mentioned this to anyone else?'

'I did say something to Mr. Kent,' she replied, 'but not as much as I have told you. I didn't say whom it was I suspected.' She paused, twisting a lacy wisp of handkerchief in her fingers nervously. 'It's — it's dreadful, isn't it?'

He nodded slowly, looking at her with troubled eyes. 'Terrible,' he agreed. 'Are you sure about the charm?'

She shook her head. 'No, not quite,' she answered. 'That's why I haven't said anything before.'

He was thoughtful, stroking his firm chin, and she watched him anxiously. She was glad now that she had confided in this man. His calmness and self-reliance, and the air of quiet strength about him, were soothing to her overstrained nerves. She had often seen him when she had called into Scotland Yard on a visit to Sir Richard, and once the chief commissioner had introduced them. She had liked him then, and admired his appearance and undoubted good looks; and, at odd moments after, had often thought about him and wondered at herself for doing so. Until now, however, they had never exchanged more than two or three words of greeting, and sometimes only a nod in passing.

'Supposing you could see it?' he asked suddenly. 'Would you be certain then?'

'I'm sure I should,' she said emphatically.

'I'll get a man down in the morning to open the safe,' he said. 'I'd get him down tonight if it wasn't for the telephone being out of order, and the fog.' He pursed his lips thoughtfully, and there was admiration in his eyes. 'So that's why the key disappeared,' he muttered almost to himself. 'What a clever devil. He thinks of everything.'

He looked at Sonia's strained white face, and his heart ached. He would cheerfully have given anything in the world to have saved her from even momentary unhappiness. For ever since the first time he had seen her, she had held a place in his thoughts that had been occupied by no other woman. And although he had spent many weary hours telling himself that he was a fool, and something more than a fool, the fact that she had become the predominant interest in his life was forced home to him even against his will.

Her voice broke in on his thoughts, and he started. 'It's almost impossible to believe that anyone could be so — so callous,' she said doubtfully.

'Why?' he answered, wrenching his mind back to the matter at hand with an effort. 'When a man has committed one murder and found no cause for remorse, he thinks nothing of a second or a third. Murder begets murder; it's like lying in that respect. You tell one lie, and you have to follow it with several more to cover up the first. The same thing applies to murder. The Shadow doesn't care how many people he kills, so long as his own safety is assured. Why should he? He knows that if he's caught he can only be hanged once.'

'Of course I may be mistaken after all,' Sonia muttered hopefully. 'It seems so awful to suspect — '

He stopped her with a gesture. 'No names, Miss Lane,' he warned, with a quick glance towards the closed door. 'Sound carries very easily, and you don't know who may be listening.' He came over to her side. 'We've got to go carefully over this, very carefully. We dare not make a move until we've got absolute proof.'

'Surely the handkerchief is sufficient proof,' she said, but he shook his head.

'Not to make an arrest, I'm afraid,' he answered, leaning against the edge of the table and gripping it with his hands. 'Up to now it's his one mistake — or rather I should say his second. The charm was his first, and he's doing his best to rectify that. We can only hope that he'll make another. In the meanwhile there's nothing to do but wait.'

He paused for a moment and looked at her steadily. 'I want you to treat him the same as you've always done,' he said earnestly, and then as she made a little impatient movement, 'I know it's difficult, but it's necessary — and above all, I don't want him to suspect that you've told me anything.'

She was silent, playing with the ring on her finger, and the light from the chandelier struck gleams of gold from her hair. Carr felt a sudden insane longing to take her in his arms and comfort her; to rest that shining gold-capped head on his shoulder and kiss away the trouble that dimmed the blue of her eyes.

'It's this uncertainty that's the worst,' she said presently. 'If only we knew, it wouldn't be so bad.' She raised her head, and the expression she surprised in his eyes brought a faint flush to her pale cheeks.

'I know,' he answered as she looked away quickly. 'But at the moment we've got to be patient. A false move might spoil — ' He stopped abruptly and jerked his head round towards the door as there came the sound of stumbling steps in the hall, and the mutter of voices. 'That sounds like Davis,' he said quickly. 'What's happened now, I wonder.'

He went hurriedly across to the door and pulled it open. Sergeant Davis was standing at the top of the stairs leading down to the kitchen, grasping by the arm a mud-stained, dishevelled, and very angry man who was arguing loudly. The plainclothes man looked round as Carr came out of the dining room.

'I found this fellow, sir,' he explained, 'trying to get back through the window in the passage.'

'This is an outrage!' broke in the prisoner, struggling violently to free himself from the sergeant's grip. 'I shall speak to Sir Richard.'

'You can,' cut in the inspector, 'but you'll speak to me first! Your name's Silverton, isn't it?'

'It is, and I demand — ' began the other, but again Carr interrupted him.

'Well then, Mr. Silverton, perhaps you'll kindly explain what you've been doing,' he snapped. 'I gave orders that no one was to leave this house.'

'I know,' growled Silverton, 'but — '

'Then why did you go out?'

'I — I had a headache,' replied the other sullenly. His face was still flushed with anger, but he was obviously trying to subdue his temper.

'I never knew mud was a good cure before,' retorted Carr sarcastically. 'How did you get in that state?' He pointed to the stains on Silverton's coat and trousers.

'I slipped and fell down,' was the ungracious answer.

'You slipped and fell down,' repeated Carr. 'I see.' He walked up to the man and stared him full in the face. 'Now listen to me, Mr. Silverton,' he said in an ominously quiet voice. 'A man doesn't take the trouble to stealthily leave a house by climbing through a window, and walk about in a thick fog to cure a headache.'

Silverton glared at him with hate-filled eyes. 'I've told you — ' he began.

'A lot of lies!' rapped the inspector. 'I want the truth. Where have you been, and what have you been doing?'

The man's face set obstinately. 'I've already told you,' he repeated.

'And I've told you I don't believe you.' Carr looked at the other narrowly. 'There's a mystery about you,' he said, frowning thoughtfully. 'I've seen you somewhere before, but I can't recollect where. Your name wasn't Silverton then, though.' His tone changed suddenly and became more brusque. 'Now, for the last time, are you going to tell me what you were doing outside to get yourself covered in mud?'

The defiant look on Silverton's face deepened. 'I've said all I'm going to say,' he answered. 'You've no right to question me as though I were a criminal.'

'We'll see about that tomorrow,' said Carr grimly. 'Davis, take Mr. Silverton up to his room. Willit will tell you which one it is. Lock the door and bring me the key.'

Silverton's face twitched, and for a moment his eyes reflected the panic that had suddenly gripped him. 'Does this mean that I'm under arrest?' he demanded.

'Not yet, officially,' answered the inspector. 'But if you try any more open-air cures you will be!'

'You are exceeding your duty,' snarled the other, his face livid with rage. 'I shall have a lot to say to your superiors about this.'

'Write it!' snapped Carr impatiently. 'At the moment you will go with Sergeant

Davis. Take him away, Davis.' He jerked his head towards the staircase.

'What about my sister?' began Silverton over his shoulder as Davis hustled him across the hall. 'Can I — '

'You needn't worry about her,' broke in Carr coolly. 'I'm locking her in as well.'

'You'll be sorry for this,' grunted the other, almost speechless with suppressed rage.

'If I am, I'll let you know,' retorted the inspector, and he turned away.

Sonia, who had watched the scene from the open door of the dining room, came over to his side. 'What do you think he went out for?'

'I don't know.' He shrugged his shoulders. 'Whatever it was, it wasn't what he said.' His forehead wrinkled in an irritated frown. 'I wish I could remember where I've seen him before. His face is terribly familiar, but I can't place him.'

The vague memory kept recurring to him at intervals for the remainder of the evening, but that night of terror was almost over before he found the answer.

15

Interlude

Dinner that evening, to at least one person seated at the long table, seemed endless. It could not by any stretch of imagination be called a cheerful meal, although Reginald Stimpson and Mrs. Bascombe made a voluble if vain effort to keep the conversation alive. In the end, however, they were reduced to talking to each other, for Sir Richard was morose and silent, and answered only in monosyllables.

Sonia, too, was occupied with her own thoughts — rather gloomy ones, to judge from the expression of her face — and kept her eyes fixed for the most part on her plate. Carr ate absently, watching her from under his drawn brows, and sympathising with the reason that had brought the worried look to her pale face. If she were right in what she had told him, there was good reason for her worry. He was worried himself, but not from the same cause. His worry lay in the coming night and what it would bring forth. The Shadow must realise that he was in danger. Even though he might not be aware of Sonia's suspicions, he must know that the opening of the safe would practically seal his doom.

So Carr, too, was silent and gloomy, concentrating on his plans for circumventing any effort that the unknown might make. The Silvertons' and Beverley Kent's dinners were taken up to them by one of the plainclothes men. When the miserable meal was over, Carr drew Sir Richard aside. He had already explained to that greatly worried man the reason for the action he had taken in regard to the Silvertons, and the chief commissioner thoroughly endorsed this action.

'Do you think,' he said when Carr and he were alone in the study, 'that this man Silverton can be the Shadow after all?'

'It's impossible to tell,' answered the young inspector. 'Tomorrow I shall instigate enquiries concerning him. In the meanwhile, do you think your secretary is sufficiently recovered for me to see him?'

'Yes, I should think so,' answered Sir Richard. 'I'll come up with you.'

He led the way out into the hall and up the staircase, and going along the right hand corridor paused outside a door at the end. At this he tapped gently, and a voice from inside muttered an invitation to enter.

Beverley Kent, looking rather pale, and with a bandage round his head, was lying on the bed, propped up by pillows. He was still fully dressed, and the tray on which his dinner had been brought to him was still on the small table at the bedside. He greeted them with rather a rueful grin.

'Come to visit the interesting invalid?' he asked. 'I was just thinking of coming down.'

'As a matter of fact I've come to ask you one or two questions, Mr. Kent,' said Carr. 'What can you tell us about this attack that was made on you?'

Beverley Kent frowned and shook his head gently. 'Very little, I'm afraid,' he answered. 'All I can remember is going up the stairs and starting to walk along the corridor towards Sir Richard's room. I heard somebody come up behind me and was turning to see who it was, when it suddenly seemed as if the whole house had collapsed. I don't recollect anything more until I came to my senses in my own room.'

'You didn't manage to catch a glimpse of your assailant?' asked Carr, and again the secretary shook his head.

'No,' he said. 'I wish I had. I just caught sight of a man's figure in the gloom and then I was out!'

'You must have disturbed him while he was lying in wait for me,' said the inspector. 'I think you're lucky that he let you off so lightly.'

The invalid grimaced. 'I don't know about lightly,' he grumbled. 'He hit me pretty hard, I can assure you. Gave me the worst headache I've ever had in my life.'

'I mean you're lucky that you're still alive,' said Carr. 'He must have been pretty sure that you hadn't seen him, or you wouldn't be.'

'I'm convinced there's someone in the house whom we've never seen,' broke in Sir Richard. 'The person Mrs. Bascombe saw looking in the window, and whose face Sunny touched on the staircase.'

Carr pursed his lips. 'If there is, he's learnt the trick of making himself invisible,' he declared. 'I've searched the house from top to bottom, and I'm prepared to swear that nothing smaller than a mouse could have escaped me.'

In this he was speaking the truth, but there was one place in Green Lanes that he had omitted to search, and that was the roof. Had he done so, he would not have been so emphatic in declaring that there was no stranger in the place.

'The whole thing's utterly impossible,' muttered the chief commissioner. 'And the more you try to think it out, the worse it becomes. Why should the Shadow be here at all? That's what I can't understand. What brought him here in the first place? It's the last place anyone would expect him to go.'

'Perhaps that's just the reason why he's

here, sir,' suggested Carr.

'There's something in that,' said Sir Richard, but his tone suggested that he didn't think there was. 'Well, I suppose we can't do more than we're doing. But I wish we could clear up this business.'

'Not more than I do,' said the young inspector, thinking of Sonia downstairs. 'There's nothing more you can tell us at all, Mr. Kent?'

'Nothing,' answered the secretary. 'I've told you all I can. If you care for a suggestion, though, I should keep an eye on that fellow Silverton. I'm rather suspicious of him.'

'Have you got any reason for saying that?' asked Carr quickly.

'No,' answered Kent, 'except instinct. I don't mind telling you that I took a dislike to him the moment I saw him. He's the only stranger in this house, and personally I don't believe his explanation as to why he's here.'

'You mean the car breaking down?' said Sir Richard. 'I must admit that after what's happened, it does look a trifle suspicious.'

The young inspector frowned. 'Every-thing about Silverton is suspicious,' he said. 'But to believe that he's the Shadow, you're still up against the ridiculous idea that he should walk into the very place where it was most dangerous for him to be.'

'He told Mrs. Bascombe he was a broker,' said Kent. 'If he was telling the truth, it should be quite easy to find out.'

'There won't be any difficulty in proving that,' agreed Carr. 'In the meanwhile, I think he's pretty safe where he is.'

The secretary looked at him question-ingly, and Sir Richard, rather to Carr's annoyance, told him about Silverton's excursion through the window. Beverley Kent whistled. 'There you are!' he said. 'That shows there's something fishy about him.'

'I'm sure there is,' said Carr. 'But at the same time, if he's the Shadow, once having got away, why did he come back? It seems to me rather a stupid thing to do.'

'Probably the fog was thicker than he

thought,' suggested Sir Richard. 'I'm pretty sure that if he isn't the Shadow himself, he's closely connected with him.'

Carr neither agreed with nor refuted this suggestion. 'Whether he is or not, sir,' he said, 'he can't do much damage where he is, and tomorrow we'll know all about him.'

He left Sir Richard still talking to his secretary, and went round and interviewed the men he had left on guard. Everything at the moment, apparently, was quite peaceful. No one had attempted either to come in or to go out. The fog was still thick, and Carr cursed below his breath as he saw that there was no sign of it dispersing.

He had a consultation with Inspector Wallace, of the local police, and roughly outlined his suggestions for the coming night. 'I think there's likely to be trouble,' he said. 'I may be wrong, but I think we'll see some fresh developments.'

The local man looked at him curiously. 'Have you discovered anything new?' he asked.

'I have, and I haven't,' said Carr

shortly. 'But be on your guard, Wallace.'

The rest of the evening passed slowly and rather monotonously. There was an atmosphere of unrest about the place, and a tension that seemed to affect them all. Even Willit looked drawn and haggard as he went about his duties.

Mrs. Bascombe was the first to go to bed, and she was followed shortly after by Reginald Stimpson. Carr was left alone for a moment in the drawing-room with Sonia, and he took advantage of the opportunity to put into words something that had been troubling him during the latter part of the evening.

'Where is your room, Miss Lane?' he asked.

'On the second landing,' she answered, 'next to Mrs. Bascombe's.'

'I'll put one of the men on guard outside your door,' he said seriously. 'And you'd better take this.' He pulled an automatic pistol from his pocket and held it out to her. 'Do you know how to use it?'

'Yes, I learnt last year.' She looked at him, rather astonished. 'I'm supposed to be quite a good shot.'

'Fine,' he replied. 'Don't hesitate to use it if necessary.'

Her fingers closed round the weapon as she took it from his hand, her eyes clouded with fear. 'Do you think it will be necessary?' she asked in a whisper.

'I hope not,' he answered sincerely, 'but it's no use disguising the fact that you're in danger.'

She caught her breath quickly.

'I'm telling you this because I think you ought to know it. So far as the Shadow is concerned, you are the only person who is a menace to his safety, and you can bet your life that his brain is working at express speed to try and remove that menace. Bolt your windows and lock your door.'

'Do you think,' she said in the same low tone, 'that he knows what I suspect?'

'I'm allowing that he does,' he answered, 'though he may not — it's impossible to say. But I think it's better to conclude that he does know, and take precautions accordingly.'

Before he could say any more, Sir

Richard came in. 'Aren't you going to bed, child?' he asked when he saw his daughter.

'Yes,' she replied, 'I'm going now.' She turned to Carr and held out her hand, and he noticed that the other one in which she was holding the automatic she kept concealed in the folds of her dress. 'Good night, Mr. Carr,' she said softly.

'Good night,' he answered. 'And don't worry. A lot may happen before morning.'

He held her hand a little longer than was strictly necessary, and it was a little reluctantly that she withdrew her fingers from his firm clasp.

'I'll see you as far as your room, Miss Lane,' he said.

'It's all right, Carr,' said Sir Richard. 'I'm going up myself now. I'll go with her.'

The young inspector looked at him steadily. 'Then we'll walk one on each side, if you don't mind, sir,' he answered. 'The corridors are dark and shadows are dangerous.'

They accompanied Sonia upstairs, and after she had closed her door Carr waited until he heard the key turn in the lock before he went in search of Larch, and posted him on guard.

'You're not to move from this position all night,' were his final instructions. 'No matter what happens. You understand?' The man nodded, and Carr went back to the hall.

Curiously enough, it was not the Shadow that was occupying his thoughts at that moment; though he was soon to, to the exclusion of everything else. For when the young inspector had told Sonia that a lot might happen before morning, he had unwittingly spoken prophetically. Before the sun rose, death was again to stalk through the silent rooms at Green Lanes, and in its passing clear up at least part of the mystery that lurked in the fog-shrouded house of the chief commissioner.

16

A Shock for Mr. Stimpson

Beverley Kent stirred uneasily on his pillow. His head was aching badly, and although he had tried every conceivable position, he could not get comfortable. He reached out and helped himself to a cigarette from the case on the table by his side, but before he had smoked half of it he discovered that was not what he wanted at all, and crushed it out irritably in the ashtray. His throat was rather dry, and he suddenly decided that the thing he wanted more than anything else was a drink; something long and cool.

He was still fully clothed, except for his collar and tie. He got up a little unsteadily and, wrapping his dressing gown round him, went over to the door. The house was very still, and he concluded that although it was barely half past eleven, everybody must have gone to bed.

Making his way down to the dining room, he pushed open the door, switched on the light, and went over to the sideboard. Pouring some gin into a glass, he filled it up with soda and swallowed the cooling drink gratefully.

As he was crossing the hall to go back to his room, he saw Stimpson coming down the stairs. Reggie looked rather surprised at seeing him, and raised his eyebrows. 'Hello, old boy. Got up?' he asked.

'Yes,' answered Kent. 'I felt thirsty and came down for a drink.'

Stimpson peered about him. 'Everybody gone to bed?' he said, and when the secretary nodded: 'Including the priceless old detective johnny?'

'I suppose so,' answered Kent. 'Even detectives have to sleep. I'm going myself in a minute, and I should advise you to do the same. I don't suppose any of us will get a moment's peace tomorrow.'

'Come into the drawing room and have a cigarette before you go,' said Stimpson. 'Dash it all, it's early yet!'

The secretary felt like refusing. He was

not particularly fond of Stimpson's company at any time, and just now, with his head throbbing and feeling anything but well, he did not relish the idea of listening to the other's inane chatter. But Reggie was already on the way to the drawing room, and feeling that perhaps it would be a little churlish to refuse, Kent shrugged his shoulders.

'You know,' said Stimpson, offering the other a cigarette and helping himself, 'I'm decidedly disappointed in this fellow Carr, old boy! He's not my idea of a sleuth at all.' He shook his head vigorously. 'I shall have to speak to Sir Richard about it in the morning. This going to bed, you know, is all wrong! Absolutely! Detectives don't do it, old chappie, they don't really.'

'What do you expect him to do?' demanded Kent. 'Sit up all night and play the violin?'

'No.' Stimpson was very serious. 'But he ought to be on the prowl. Things always happen in the night. The jolly old criminal comes forth thinking he's got the house to himself, and that everyone's asleep. And then just as he's going to — to commit some fiendish and carefully planned crime, the detective johnny pops his head out between the window curtains, or — or somewhere like that, and says, 'Hands up!' The crook gets a fearful shock, and — and there you are!'

Kent laughed. 'You do talk a lot of rot!' he said.

Mr. Stimpson looked a little hurt. 'Oh I say, old boy,' he protested in an injured voice, 'that's — that's rude, you know.'

'It's the truth, anyway,' retorted the secretary, but the other shook his head.

'It's not rot at all. I've put that situation into my stories ever so many times.'

Kent made a grimace. 'That doesn't make it any the less idiotic,' he replied.

'Well anyway,' said Stimpson, 'I've a jolly good mind to — to stay up myself, what! I'm jolly sure something will happen before the dawn.'

'I'm sure,' said Kent, strolling over to the door. 'Personally I'm going to bed. If I meet the Shadow I'll tell him you're in the drawing room.'

His hand was on the handle when it

was pushed open from outside and Mrs. Bascombe peeped in. 'Oh, it's you, is it?' she said, entering and clutching the folds of a filmy negligée about her. 'I thought I heard the sound of voices. How is your poor head, Mr. Kent? We were all so *dreadfully* sorry to hear about it, but really I think the bandage suits you!'

'I'm feeling much better, thank you, Mrs. Bascombe,' said the secretary politely.

'I'm *so* glad,' she answered. 'I wish I could say the same, but my poor nerves are really in a dreadful state, and everybody's been *so* unsympathetic. I *do* think a little sympathy goes such a long way, don't you?'

'I should think a long sleep would be far better myself,' answered Kent.

She looked at him pathetically. 'I wish I *could* sleep,' she said with a sigh. 'I've tried, but I can't. It's completely out of the question. The mere thought of being alone in my room with all these dreadful things happening makes me shudder all over. With my disposition, you know, I was never intended to be alone. That's why I miss poor, dear George so. He was such wonderful company. Not that he ever talked much.'

'By jove!' remarked Stimpson, 'I can quite believe that, what!'

Mrs. Bascombe gave him a sweet smile. 'You *would* understand, of course, Mr. Stimpson,' she said. 'I always think that anyone who is at all artistic is so much more sensitive to the feelings of others than an ordinary person. It's the temperament, you know. I'm so full of it myself. My father — he's dead now, poor dear — was hanged in the Royal Academy — '

'Well, I'm going to bed,' interrupted Kent, as she took a deep breath preparatory to going on. 'If you two people like to stop up all night, it's your affair.'

'Take Mrs. Bascombe with you,' said Stimpson hastily. 'I mean, see her to her room. She must be fearfully tired and all that.' He made frantic signs behind her back.

'I'm not a teeny little bit sleepy, I assure you,' said that lady. 'Poor, dear George was always thinking of others, just like that. I remember once just after our marriage, I was laid up with an attack of influenza, and my mother came to nurse me. He *insisted* upon going to live at a hotel in case he should be in the way. I thought it was *so* nice of him.'

'Very nice *for* him!' said Stimpson.

'Well, good night,' remarked Kent, opening the door. 'Pleasant dreams, Mrs. Bascombe.'

'Here, I say!' said Reggie frantically. 'Don't go yet, old boy!'

'My dear chap, I'm tired,' said the secretary, and added with a touch of malice: 'If you want someone to keep watch with you, I'm sure Mrs. Bascombe will be only too pleased!'

He went out hurriedly, closing the door behind him, and Mrs. Bascombe turned with a beaming smile to the speechless Stimpson. 'What does he mean about keeping watch?' she said. 'Do tell me.'

'Well you see, old thing — er, I beg your pardon,' answered Reggie uncomfortably. 'It's like this. The detective fellow, and everyone else, seem to have toddled off to close the weary peeper, as it were, and I think that someone ought to be about, in case this Shadow johnny takes it into his head to start something, what?'

'And were *you* going to stop up all by yourself?' she asked admiringly. 'How brave of you! I *adore* brave men! Of course, I'll stay, too. It'll be so thrilling, won't it?'

Stimpson's jaw dropped. 'I — I don't think you ought to do that, you know,' he said. 'It's fearfully risky. You don't know what might happen!'

She came a little closer to him. 'I know that whatever happens,' she said softly, 'I can rely upon you to take care of me.'

'Oh, yes, you're quite safe with me!' he said, backing away. 'But I — I really think you ought to go to bed.' He searched frantically for some excuse, and then a happy thought struck him. 'You must look after yourself, you know; consider your appearance and all that. Nothing spoils a woman's beauty more than loss of sleep!'

'Really, you know, I never thought of that,' she said, and he gave a sigh of relief.

'Of course, you're quite right. I suppose I really ought to try and get a little rest. But I don't like leaving you here all alone.'

'Oh, I shall be quite all right,' he said, escorting her gently but firmly towards the door in case she should change her mind. 'You — you go to bed and forget all about everything.'

She gave him a charming smile. 'I will,' she answered. 'I think it's terribly sweet of you.' She waved to him coquettishly, and went out.

He closed the door after her and came back into the centre of the room. For a moment he stood frowning down at the carpet; and then, going over to the window, he pulled back the curtains, opened it, and looked out. He failed to see the door slowly open and a hand reach in and search for the light switch. He was just turning back from the window when all the lights in the room went out!

Mr. Stimpson's breath left his lungs in a gasp. 'By jove!' he quavered. 'I say, who's that? D-d-don't do anything silly, you know!'

As suddenly as they had gone out, the lights came on again. Willit was standing just inside the door, his hand on the switch. 'I'm sorry, sir,' he said. 'I didn't mean to startle you. I thought everyone had gone to bed.'

With a shaking hand, Mr. Stimpson took his handkerchief from his pocket and dabbed at his moist face. 'Oh, it's — it's you, Willit, is it?' he muttered a little breathlessly. 'W-What were you doing with those lights?'

'Putting them out, sir,' answered the butler.

'Why?' demanded Reggie, and Willit looked rather surprised.

'I usually do, sir, before I retire for the night,' he replied.

'Yes, of course you do,' said Mr. Stimpson shakily. 'I — I see. You thought the — the room was empty, what?'

'Yes, sir.' The butler bowed. 'I'm sorry I frightened you.'

Stimpson was recovering a little from his shock. 'Oh, you didn't frighten me!' he said, shaking his head. 'Not for a moment. As a matter of fact, it was jolly lucky for you that you put the lights on again as quickly as you did. In another second I should have tackled you!'

'Indeed, sir?' Willit's lips quivered, but he checked the smile. 'If you are remaining up, I'll wish you good night, sir.'

He turned towards the door, but Reggie stopped him. 'On second thoughts, Willit,' he said hastily, 'I think I'll go to bed after all. It's — it's getting deuced cold, you know.' He came over to the butler's side. 'Night, night, old chappie. See you in the morning.'

'I hope so, sir,' said Willit stolidly.

With one foot across the threshold, Stimpson stopped abruptly. 'Eh?' he said, looking round. 'You — you don't seem very certain about it, what?'

Willit shook his head. 'It's impossible to be certain about anything, sir,' he answered. 'With all these goings-on in the house, one doesn't know what may happen.'

'By jove!' Reggie looked at him, his mouth half-open. 'You don't think that — that anything's going to happen to me, do you?'

'It wouldn't surprise me in the least, sir,' said the butler gravely.

'Oh, it — it wouldn't, eh?' Reggie's hand went up to his lips. 'You're a perfectly priceless old optimist, aren't you? I'm jolly well going to my room, and I shall lock the door!'

He hurried away, and Willit heard him going up the stairs two at a time. For a moment the butler stood looking after him, and then putting out the drawing room lights, he, too began to ascend the big staircase.

17

Night!

Mrs. Bascombe sat before the mirror in her bedroom and carefully examined her face. She smiled complacently at the reflection in the glass, unaware that age had dimmed her eyesight and that what she saw was but a memory of what had been. And so she smiled. Her smile revealed the white, even teeth that were a tribute to the art of her dentist, and also brought into prominence the dimples at either side of her mouth which were the only surviving attributes of the girlhood she was so reluctant to put behind her. She leaned closer and studied her eyes with interest. There were little lines spreading from the corners, and a suspicion of puffiness beneath.

She glanced at the pots of cream and bottles of lotion that littered the top of the dressing table. It was time for her to start her usual hour's massage, during which, with the tips of her fingers, she tried to smooth and pat away the wrinkles which time was nightly making more difficult to eradicate. But tonight for some reason she was loath to begin this task. Perhaps at the back of her small mind she had some idea that if there should be an alarm while her face was shining with cream, she would be at a disadvantage. Anyway, her hand straying towards a scented jar was stayed. Instead, she sat and continued to stare at her reflection in the soft lights that flanked the mirror. She had worn well, she thought with satisfaction. There was little sign of the age which she dreaded.

It seemed incredible that Sir Richard could be so blind to her attractions. It wasn't as if she hadn't given him every encouragement. Perhaps when all this fuss and bother over the Shadow was finished, he would take more notice of her. How sweet it had been of Reggie Stimpson to insist that she should get her proper rest. He was quite a nice boy at times. Perhaps if Sir Richard failed to come up to her expectations . . .

She gave a little sigh and fluttered her lashes. It was a habit she practised assiduously. She practised all her mannerisms before her mirror. There was not a gesture or an expression that was not studiously cultivated and rehearsed. She was artificial to the core. There was nothing real about her, from her painted face and dyed hair to her mean, vain little soul. For a few more years she would flutter and chatter and massage, and then her fluttering and her chattering would be still forever, and all the lotions and creams in the world would be of no avail . . .

★　★　★

Beverley Kent shifted the bandage gingerly round his forehead, lit a cigarette, and sat down on the side of his bed. He made no effort to undress, but sat smoking thoughtfully and staring at nothing in particular. Presently a faint smile curled the corners of his mouth as he thought of Stimpson and Mrs.

Bascombe together in the drawing room. What a fool the fellow was, and what an awful bore she was. Ugly as sin, and old as the devil, and still under the delusion that she was attractive. A brainless chatterbox, almost as big an idiot as Stimpson himself, and that was saying something. If they *did* stop up, it would almost serve them right if . . .

The smile vanished and was replaced by a frown as a fresh thought came to him. Had that fellow Carr really gone to bed? Unconsciously he shook his head in answer to the unspoken question. Much more likely he wanted everybody to think so, and was about somewhere. He was on to something. Quite a clever fellow in his way. Well, he'd have to be a jolly sight cleverer than the rest of them, if he were going to catch the Shadow . . . Perhaps Sonia had told him something. That had been rather a shock. He would have liked to have known whom it was she really suspected . . . Where could she have seen that charm before? He lighted another cigarette, although he had crushed out the other before it was half-smoked; and, rising to his feet, he went over to the window and looked out.

★ ★ ★

Sonia lay staring up into the darkness that shrouded her room. She was very tired, but her mind was too active for sleep. Her thoughts came and went almost without meaning, a chaotic jumble through which the knowledge she possessed concerning the charm ran like the main motif in a musical symphony. If the fog cleared in the morning, the safe would be opened, and her doubts and fears and conjectures would be resolved into a certainty one way or the other. One way or the other? Which way? She hoped with all her heart that she was wrong; it would be dreadful if she were right, and yet she wanted desperately to know. The uncertainty was nerve-wracking.

Her thoughts began to centre on the young detective. She wondered what had at first turned his attention to the police force as a career. He must at one time have walked a beat as a constable, and she smiled as she pictured him patrolling majestically along a London street. She was still thinking of Carr when all thoughts ran out of her head and she fell asleep.

* * *

The man called Silverton paced softly up and down his room, his fingers at his mouth, gnawing at his nails. He made no sound, walking with a catlike tread, and pausing every now and again to stare at the communicating door which separated him from Moya. He was in a nasty mess, and he knew it. Unless he could get out of it before morning, it would mean his finish. Curse the fog and the blasted car! The two things together had combined to bring about this catastrophe. Moya had been right that day when he had discussed his plans with her. She must have had some form of second sight . . . or was it just intuition?

Anyway, it was no good thinking about that. He would need to concentrate all his attention on finding a way out of this unpleasant situation. By hook or by crook he must get away before the morning. He had taken what precautions he could, but once the fog cleared his danger would be increased a hundred-fold. If they found those things he had so carefully hidden, it would be all up. He took out his cigarette case, and with fingers that shook, helped himself to a cigarette and sat down on the side of the bed, smoking savagely. He could hear a movement outside his door and guessed that one of the detectives had been put there on guard. It was useless therefore to consider that as a means of escape. The only thing that remained was the window. Was there any chance of getting out that way? He continued to sit smoking and thinking for a long time, and presently he began to evolve a plan . . .

*   *   *

Reginald Stimpson brushed his hair carefully. He had undressed, and was clad only in pyjamas and a dressing gown. What had happened to Carr? It was jolly silly if he had really gone to bed — a most stupid thing to do. Surely he must realise that if the Shadow were contemplating anything, the night was the time he would choose to put his schemes into practice? No wonder they'd never succeeded in catching him, if this was the usual way the police went to work. By jove, he could have taught them a thing or two . . .

What was the matter with Willit? Sonia had been quite right when she had mentioned the change in the butler. There *was* something peculiar about him. Since her remark he had watched him carefully, and there was a frightened look about him. Did he know anything? He paused in his hair-brushing and stared into the mirror with a slightly open mouth. Perhaps that was the reason. And the sneaky way he had come into the drawing room a few minutes before . . . Yes, there was something peculiar going on. His light eyebrows drew together in a frown, and he stood for some time, a brush in each hand, staring thoughtfully at the mirror in front of him. Presently he shrugged his shoulders, put the brushes carefully in their case, switched out the light and got into bed.

* * *

Sir Richard paced his bedroom thoughtfully, his hands clasped behind his back, his chin sunk forward on his chest. He was feeling vaguely uneasy. There was something going on of which he was unaware; Carr knew something which he hadn't told him. He had seen it in one or two fleeting expressions that had crossed the man's face. What *was* it that Carr knew or suspected, that he was keeping to himself? It was very worrying, and he was worried enough without having any extra put upon him. Although he had been in his room for some time, he had not yet started to undress, but was still fully clothed as he had been when he came upstairs.

That last remark of the young inspector's was still rankling in his mind. Why had he been so insistent on accompanying Sonia as far as her room? It almost looked as though he were afraid of trusting her with her father. The chief commissioner stopped suddenly. Surely he couldn't suspect . . . His face went a little pale. No, it was out of the question. At the same time, Carr was behaving very strangely. He shrugged his shoulders. All this thinking and wondering would do no good. He locked the door, pulled the curtains across the window, and began his preparations for the night.

★　★　★

The Shadow thought coolly and calmly. He had a lot to do before the dawn, and it must be done carefully. That charm must be retrieved from the safe. He had the keys, and it was only a question of getting into the library and out again without being discovered, which he didn't think should be too difficult. But he must choose his time; it was too early yet. He began carefully to prepare for his coming excursion.

18

The Man Who Was Killed

Carr stationed his men carefully before he finally settled down to snatch a few hours' rest. When everyone had finally gone to bed, he called Davis from the back exit, substituting in his place Inspector Wallace from the front. One of the constables who had been patrolling round the outside of the house he brought in, and stationed him between the doors of the two Silvertons' rooms. When he had done this, he went the round of all the lower windows to see that they were fastened, and finally took up his position on a heap of rugs by the front door.

From here he could command a view of the library and the dining room doors, both of which he had locked, and the hall, in which he had left one electric light burning. The passage that led round to the barred iron door was hidden from him, as was also the foot of the stairs; but since that exit would have taken the best part of an hour to break open, he was not troubling about it much.

Curling himself up, he drew a rug about him and waited. The house was very still, except for an occasional creak from the old woodwork. He wondered if the fog would be gone by the morning, and hoped that it would. His first task would be to get somebody down from London who could open the safe. That would resolve all doubts, and prove whether Sonia was right in her suspicions.

His thoughts turned to her very readily; it was foolish, but he rather liked the foolishness. It was absurd, of course, but he thought that he had seen something in her eyes when she had said good night that was more than friendliness. Perhaps the wish was father to the thought. Perhaps he had imagined that momentary expression as he held her hand. Anyway, she was the daughter of the chief commissioner, and he was only an inspector. But if he brought this case to a successful conclusion, there might be a chance of promotion. Even then . . . Still, it was nice to dream, and it didn't hurt anyone except the dreamer when he woke up.

The warmth of the blanket in which he had wrapped himself was beginning to make him feel drowsy. He yawned . . . He was very tired . . . Presently breathing softly and silently, he slept. Half an hour passed slowly, and then among the gloomy shadows at the head of the big staircase appeared a darker shadow. It paused, listening; and, turning, beckoned into the darkness behind it. A second figure loomed out of the gloom; and cautiously and stealthily, making no sound on the thick carpet, the two began to make their way noiselessly down the stairs. Reaching the hall, the first stopped and, raising a warning hand, peered about him. In the dim rays of the single electric bulb, Willit's face looked white and anxious.

He eyed the shadowy form of the sleeping inspector fearfully, then put his finger to his lips as he took his muffled companion by the arm and led him round to the passage that ended in the iron door. Outside the door leading from this into the library the butler halted and, feeling in his pocket, produced a key with which he softly unlocked the door. Silently he ushered the man with him into the darkened room, followed him in, and closing the door behind him relocked it.

'You'd better get away now while you've got the chance,' he whispered in an unsteady voice, speaking with his lips close to the other's ear. 'The house will be swarming with detectives and police in the morning, and you're sure to be found if you stop here. It's a wonder you haven't been already. You would if they'd thought of looking on the roof.'

The muffled man nodded. 'I thought it was all up when I banged into that woman on the stairs,' he replied, and his voice was rough and uneducated.

'It would have been if I hadn't put the hall light out,' said Willit huskily. 'You shouldn't have left the roof. I had trouble enough to get you up there, for I knew that Inspector Carr would want to search the linen cupboard.'

'Blast him!' growled the other viciously. 'It was 'im what got me my stretch. I'd like to get my 'ands on 'im! The — '

The butler looked round nervously. 'Sh — shh!' he muttered. 'Think yourself lucky he didn't get his hands on you.'

'It 'ud 'ave been 'ard for 'im if 'e 'ad,' was the husky reply. 'I'd never 'ave let meself be took back. You don't know the Moor — it's a livin' 'ell, that place.'

'You'd better be going,' said Willit quickly. 'You can write and let me know where you are. You've got enough money to be going on with?'

'It won't last long,' grumbled his companion. 'Is it all you've got?'

'It's all I've got in the house,' said the butler. 'I'll send you some more.' He took the other by the arm and led him towards the window.

'There must be all sorts of pickin's in a place like this,' said the muffled man suggestively. 'Why can't yer — '

Willit interrupted him with a low exclamation. 'Can't you even *think* straight?' he muttered bitterly.

'Oh, it's easy enough for you to

preach,' grunted the man hoarsely. 'You've got a good job and comfort. I've got nothin'. I don't even know where I'm goin' to from 'ere, and wherever I go the busies will be chasin' me.' He uttered an oath. 'I wish I was the Shadder.'

The butler shivered. 'He's a murderer!' he protested.

'Well, supposin' he is?' growled the other. ''E's got money, ain't 'e? And that's what counts.'

'But think what he's got on his conscience,' said the old man.

His companion gave a harsh laugh, and the butler looked round in sudden panic. 'Conscience!' snarled the other. 'What's the good of a conscience and an empty stomach? If I'd got 'is money I wouldn't 'ave to go and 'ide in some filthy slum, like a rat in an 'ole. I could get away abroad, and forget the sound of the prison bell, and the warders and the bloody exercise yard. I wish I knew 'oo the Shadder was; I'd go to 'im. It 'ud be worth a bit to keep me mouth shut.'

'Have you any idea who he is?' asked Willit, his curiosity getting the better of his fear of discovery for the moment.

The muffled man shook his head. 'No, I don't suppose anybody ever will know,' he answered. ''E's too clever to be caught. 'E's got a brain, that feller. I've 'eard tales about ''im up on the Moor.' He glanced round quickly. 'Well, I suppose I'd better 'ook it. I'll 'ave to lie low somewhere until this fog clears.'

'I'll send you some more money,' began the butler, and broke off as the other gripped his arm tightly.

'Shut up!' he grunted. 'What's that?' He looked towards the window; a faint sound had reached his ears. The scrape of a boot against stone!

'There's someone outside there!' he whispered fiercely; and even as he spoke, a ray of light flashed for a second against the blackness of the night. It winked and went out. Someone was outside the window — someone with a torch.

'Quick!' Willit's voice was almost incoherent with fear. 'Get behind that chair. It may be one of the detectives!'

The man hurriedly slipped behind a big easy chair that stood in a corner of the room, and the butler, his heart pounding and the perspiration streaming down his forehead, crouched at the back of the settee. They had barely concealed themselves before there came a little crack from the window, and a cold draught of air blew into the room.

A white shaft of light cut through the darkness and went dancing about in all directions. Of the person behind it, nothing could be seen but a shapeless blur. Presently the light came to rest on the door of the safe, and the intruder crossed over and knelt before it. More plainly visible now, silhouetted against the white circle on the wall, the butler saw that the newcomer was dressed in a long black coat and wore a slouch hat pulled low over the eyes.

The figure gave a little grunt of satisfaction, and began to feel in its pockets. While doing so, the torch shifted round slightly to the left, and its light fell full upon the chair behind which the muffled man was hiding. It shone for a second on the unshaven face, and staring eyes peering round the back; then it went out while the man who held it leaped to his feet with a startled oath.

'Who the hell — !'

The man behind the chair sprang up and flung himself forward, grasping at the figure in black, and the terrified butler heard them stumbling backwards and forwards in the dark, breathing heavily.

'I'm going to 'ave a look at you!' gasped the man, and for an instant the torch flashed out as he wrenched it from the other's hand. 'By God, I know you!' he cried hoarsely. 'You're — '

A sudden sharp pain caught him between the shoulder blades, a dreadful red-hot pain that seemed to envelop his whole body in one swift rush of agony. The words died in his throat, choked by the blood that was filling his mouth, and he staggered and fell with a crash that shook the room.

The figure in black made a dart for the window, wrenched it open and vanished into the fog-shrouded night. Willit, his whole body quivering, crawled over to the man on the floor.

'Jack,' he muttered brokenly. 'Jack!'

But there was no sound or movement in reply, and his groping fingers stirred no life in the silent figure. There was a shout in the hall, followed by hurried footsteps, and Carr's voice came from outside the door.

'Who's in there?' he cried sharply. The lock clicked, the door was flung open, and the young inspector stood on the threshold, his hand on the electric light switch, blinking at the scene before him in the sudden flood of light.

Willit was still crouching over the body of the roughly dressed man who lay huddled up in the middle of the floor, the blood welling from under him and spreading over the carpet in a widening pool.

'Willit!' cried Carr in astonishment. 'What are you doing here? Who's that?'

The old man turned his white face and streaming eyes towards the detective, and his lips moved, but no sound came from them.

Carr took a quick step forward and, bending down, peered at the face of the man on the floor. As he saw it he uttered a quick exclamation. 'Good God!' he cried. 'Cosher Jackson — the man who escaped from Dartmoor three weeks ago! How the devil did he get here?'

The butler's trembling lips moved again, and with an effort he succeeded in forcing himself to speak. 'He — he came to me for help,' he whispered.

The amazement on the inspector's face deepened. 'You!' he said. 'Why you?'

It was a long time before the answer came, and then: 'Because he was my son,' said Willit simply.

19

A Woman's Scream

'I always thought your son died abroad, Willit, during the war,' said Sir Richard gently.

A quarter of an hour had passed since the tragedy, and Carr had aroused the chief commissioner from sleep. He was standing now by the fireplace in the library, clad in a dressing gown over his pyjamas, facing the butler and the young detective.

Willit, sitting by the writing table, looked pale and ill, and seemed to have aged ten years since the beginning of that memorable and tragic day. The body of the ex-convict had been removed and laid beside that of Fleming in the little room at the end of the hall, a grim and silent testimony to the terror that lurked unseen about the corridors and rooms of Green Lanes.

'I let everybody think so, sir,' said the butler, raising his eyes to his master's face. 'It wouldn't have done any good to have told the truth, and I might have lost my job.'

'You had no right to have tried to hide him, Willit,' said Carr, shaking his head. 'After all, whether he was your son or not, he was an escaped convict — and a dangerous one at that.'

Willit nodded helplessly. 'I know it was wrong,' he admitted. 'But what could I do? He came to me for help and I couldn't very well turn him away. Whatever he's done, I was his father, and he promised that if he could get away this time, he would turn over a new leaf.'

'He'd never have kept his promise,' said the inspector. 'Cosher Jackson could never have run straight.'

'You may be right, sir,' answered Willit, 'but I gave him the benefit of the doubt. Jack wasn't all bad. He got mixed up with the wrong set, that's what started it, and perhaps I was a lot to blame for leaving him on his own when his mother died.' He sighed. 'Well, whatever he's done, he's paid for it now. I — I hope you'll overlook what I did, Sir Richard.'

The chief commissioner stroked his chin gently. 'You shouldn't have done it, Willit,' he said gruffly. 'But I don't see how I can blame you. Under the circumstances, I should have done the same myself.'

'Thank you, sir,' said the butler gratefully.

'What about the man who came through the window?' asked Carr. 'Would you be able to recognise him again?'

The old man shook his head. 'No, sir,' he replied. 'It was in the dark, and I never saw his face.'

'But you can give some description, surely?' urged the inspector. 'Was he tall or short?'

'It's difficult to say, sir.' Willit frowned. 'I should think he was about Sir Richard's height, sir.'

Carr's eyes half-closed for a moment. It was only an instant, a mere passing flicker, and neither of the other two noticed it. 'You say he went to the safe?' he asked abruptly, and the butler inclined his grey head.

'Yes,' he replied. 'He was examining the door when he caught sight of poor Jack.'

'Did he have any keys in his hand?' asked the inspector.

'I don't know, sir,' answered Willit. 'I couldn't see.'

Carr paused thoughtfully, biting at his lower lip. 'Jackson recognised him, didn't he?' he said at length. 'What were his exact words?'

Willit thought for a moment before replying. 'When he sprang at the man he said: 'I'm going to have a look at you.' And then he cried, 'I know you, you're — ' His voice sort of choked then, and he must have died before he could say any more.' The old man checked a sob.

'As they all have,' muttered Carr grimly. 'No one yet seems to have known the Shadow and lived.'

There was a short silence, and Carr walked across to the writing table and picked up the torch that the unknown killer had left behind.

'You ought to have that examined for fingerprints,' said the chief commissioner.

'There aren't any, sir,' replied the detective. 'He wore gloves.' He turned to the butler and held out the torch. 'Have you ever seen this before?' he asked.

Willit took it and, looking at it, started. 'Yes, sir,' he replied in a low voice.

'You have, eh?' said Carr sharply. 'Where?'

The butler hesitated and the inspector repeated his question. 'On — on Sir Richard's dressing-table, sir,' he answered reluctantly.

The commissioner gave a startled exclamation and stepped forward. 'On my dressing table?' he exclaimed incredulously. 'Let me look!'

Carr took it from the butler's hand and passed it to him. He looked at it, his face the picture of amazement.

'Good heavens!' he said. 'It *is* mine!'

Carr nodded shortly. 'I thought it might be, sir,' he said. Taking it back, he slipped it into his pocket.

'I'll swear it was in my room this afternoon,' muttered the chief commissioner, frowning heavily. 'He must have taken it when he took the keys.'

'I wonder,' remarked the inspector thoughtfully, 'why every criminal, however clever he may be, always gets caught in the end through making stupid little mistakes.'

Sir Richard stared at him. 'What do you mean?' he asked in a puzzled tone.

'The Shadow has made two,' said Carr. 'He hasn't been content to leave well alone.' Before the other could reply, he turned again to Willit. 'This man spoke, didn't he,' he asked, 'when your son recognised him?' The butler nodded. 'Did you recognise his voice?'

'No, sir.' The old man shook his head. 'But — I thought it seemed familiar, sir. I thought I'd heard it before.'

'Where?' asked Sir Richard quickly.

'I can't tell you, sir,' answered the butler. 'It was just something in the tone. I seemed to recognise it, and yet I didn't, if you understand what I mean, sir.'

'Try and think, Willit,' urged Carr. 'Was it like mine?

'No, sir, not in the least,' declared the butler.

'Like Mr. Kent's?

'No, sir, not as deep as Mr. Kent's.'

'Mr. Stimpson's, then?

'No, sir, I can't describe it, except that it seemed familiar.'

'Was it like mine, Willit?' asked the chief commissioner quietly.

'I — I can't say, sir, really.' Willit was vaguely uneasy.

'Was it like Sir Richard's?' said Carr sharply.

'It — it might have been something like, sir,' muttered the butler, and the chief commissioner shrugged his shoulders.

'You see, Carr,' he said, 'the only person whom the Shadow's voice recalls to Willit's mind is myself. And it couldn't possibly have been me. I'm afraid it proves how useless it is as a means of identifying the man.'

'Voices are deceiving, sir,' said Carr thoughtfully. 'People may try to disguise them and succeed to a certain extent, but there's always some slight intonation that creeps through. Would you recognise the voice again if you heard it, Willit?'

'I — I think I should,' answered the

butler, but he sounded by no means confident.

'I hope you'll have a chance,' said the chief commissioner. 'But I'm beginning to wonder if we shall ever catch him.'

Carr's lips curled into a smile. It was a hard smile, without a trace of mirth. 'We'll catch him all right, sir,' he said, and there was something in his voice that caused Sir Richard to look at him quickly.

'I believe you suspect someone,' he said pointedly.

'Maybe I do, sir, and maybe I don't,' answered Carr evasively, and caught his breath sharply as a shrill scream suddenly rang through the silent house. 'Merciful God!' he cried, his face grey. 'What was that?'

As he wrenched open the door, a cold hand seemed to clutch at his heart, for the scream had been that of a woman in terror!

20

Gone!

With his heart in his mouth, Carr dashed into the hall with Sir Richard close on his heels. As they came out of the library, Mrs. Bascombe came stumbling down the stairs, holding a flamboyant dressing gown around her.

'Help!' she shrieked, her eyes starting from her head. Then, catching sight of Carr, she rushed to him and almost collapsed in his arms. 'Oh, Inspector — Sir Richard!' she gasped breathlessly. 'I am so glad you're both here. I'm terrified!'

'What is it? What's the matter?' rapped Carr sharply, and his relief was great, for he had feared that it was Sonia who had screamed.

'Oh dear!' panted Mrs. Bascombe. 'I'm quite breathless — running down the stairs, you know.'

They took her into the library and seated her in a chair. 'What made you scream?' asked Sir Richard.

'I was dreadfully frightened.' She patted her dishevelled hair. 'I *do* hope I don't look a sight, but it was a terrible experience.'

'What was?' snapped Carr impatiently.

'I'm sure I wonder I didn't faint at the dreadful sight,' she rattled on. 'It only shows what willpower does for one, you know.'

'Mrs. Bascombe,' said the chief commissioner irritably, 'will you tell us what happened?'

She looked at him reproachfully. 'Isn't that what I'm doing as fast as I can?' she said. 'Really, I think you're a little unreasonable. I'm sure I've been upset enough, but I naturally thought I should be quite safe in my room, particularly since I'd locked the door and put the washstand against it — '

'Please come to the point,' broke in the inspector. 'What frightened you?'

'Oh dear, I *wish* you wouldn't flurry me so,' she said nervously. 'You're not at *all* sympathetic, and really I've had a most *dreadful* shock.'

Carr sighed helplessly and shook his head. 'Was there someone in your room?' he asked patiently.

'I'm trying to tell you,' she replied. 'But you *will* keep interrupting me.'

The inspector gave Sir Richard a despairing glance.

'I had gone to bed,' she went on, 'but I couldn't sleep. I kept wondering what was going to happen to us all, and trying to make up my mind whether I should wear my navy-blue costume or my beige silk frock tomorrow.' She broke off and turned to Sir Richard. 'Which do *you* think suits me best?' she asked archly.

'Oh, either!' he growled. 'Go on, Mrs. Bascombe!'

'I think you might take a little more interest,' she protested, 'but that's so like a man.'

'Will you continue your story?' asked Carr loudly.

'Oh, yes, where was I?' she said, screwing up her face. 'Oh, I know. Well suddenly, while I was thinking, I heard a noise over by the window.' She lowered her voice impressively. 'And there it was!'

'What?' asked Carr sharply.

'The mouse!' she replied.

He stared at her incredulously. 'The — the what?' he stammered.

'The mouse,' said Mrs. Bascombe with a shiver. 'Didn't you — '

'Good heavens, woman!' roared the chief commissioner angrily. 'Do you mean to say that you've been making all this fuss about a mouse?'

She looked at him in pained surprise. 'It was the largest mouse I've ever seen,' she asserted, 'sitting over — '

'Alicia!' Sonia entered the room hurriedly, a dressing gown over her nightdress. 'What were you screaming for?'

Carr swung round quickly at the sound of her voice. 'You shouldn't have left your room, Miss Lane,' he said. 'I told you not to under any circumstances.'

'I had to come and see what had happened,' she answered contritely. 'I couldn't stop there alone, imagining all sorts of things. What was it?' She looked from one to the other enquiringly.

'Nothing, child,' said the chief commissioner, pulling his arm round her. 'Mrs. Bascombe saw a mouse in her room and lost her head.'

'I think it's very unkind of you to speak like that,' whimpered that lady tearfully. 'I'm sure I was most brave. If you only knew how scared to death I am of mice, you'd be a little more understanding.'

Reginald Stimpson ambled into the room, his hair ruffled, and his vacuous face wearing an expression of concern. 'By jove!' he remarked disappointedly, overhearing her last words. 'Was that what all the bally row was about, eh? All over a jolly little mouse.'

Mrs. Bascombe dabbed at her eyes with a wisp of handkerchief. 'It wasn't a little mouse at all,' she said plaintively. 'It was a monster.'

Mr. Stimpson raised his eyebrows. 'Perhaps it was a rat,' he suggested. 'What colour was it — pink?'

She shook her head indignantly. 'I've never seen a pink rat,' she protested.

'Haven't you?' He appeared rather

surprised. 'They're jolly little fellows. They used to be fearfully common in America; the bootleggers bred 'em.'

'Will you all go back to your rooms now, please?' interrupted Carr sharply, and Stimpson turned at the sound of his voice, smiling blandly.

'Hello, old boy,' he said pleasantly. 'You're here, then, and fully dressed too. By jove, I owe you an apology. Do you know, I thought you'd gone to bed and left us all at the mercy of the jolly old criminal. I'm glad to find I was mistaken, old boy.'

'I thought you'd be pleased,' snapped the inspector. 'That's why I stayed up.'

'Oh, Inspector,' said Mrs. Bascombe pathetically, 'I couldn't go back and face that animal, I really couldn't. I should die of fright.'

'Couldn't we stay here, Mr. Carr?' suggested Sonia.

He hesitated, frowning. 'Well, if you do,' he answered after a pause, 'it must be on one condition: that you all stay together.'

'What's the giddy old brainwave, laddie?'

enquired Mr. Stimpson, lighting a cigarette.

'Simply that I want to know where
everybody is until I can get into
communication with the Yard,' answered
Carr. 'I don't mind whether you're all
here, or in your rooms, but if you stay
here nobody must leave this room, you
understand?

Sir Richard looked at him curiously. 'I
suppose you've got a good reason,' he
began, 'but I don't quite see — '

'I'd rather not explain now, sir, if you
don't mind,' broke in the inspector.

The chief commissioner shrugged his
shoulders. 'Well, anyway,' he said resignedly, 'I don't suppose many of us would
sleep much.'

'There's certainly *one* who wouldn't,
sir,' remarked Carr meaningfully, and he
walked over to the window. It was still
dark outside, but the yellow vapour was
rapidly thinning, giving place to a less
opaque white mist. 'The fog's clearing
already,' he said, dropping the curtain he
had pulled aside. 'In a few more hours
it'll be light.' He came back to the centre

of the room. 'Willit,' he said gently, and the butler who had been sitting with bowed head looked up. 'You'll find a constable upstairs. Ask him to come here at once, will you.' Willit rose silently, inclined his head, and left the room.

There was a long pause after he had gone; a stillness that could almost be felt. Into the atmosphere had crept a peculiar sense of tension, which was visible on the faces of everyone present. Nobody spoke until there came a tap on the door and the constable entered.

'You want me, sir?' he asked.

'Yes.' The young inspector took a key from his pocket and threw it across to the man. 'Go up and bring Mr. Silverton and his sister down.'

The policeman nodded. 'Very good, sir,' he said.

'Come with them,' ordered Carr. 'Don't let them out of your sight.'

'By jove!' remarked Mr. Stimpson excitedly, as the constable withdrew to carry out his instructions. 'This is getting frightfully mysterious, what? Are you going to give us a lecture or something?'

'No, I'm not,' said Carr shortly. 'I'm afraid you'll have to amuse yourselves until daylight.'

'I might read one of my stories,' suggested Reggie brightly. 'By jove, just the right atmosphere for *The Fourteenth Corpse*, what?'

'If you do,' said Sir Richard grimly, 'there'll be a fifteenth corpse!' The disgusted author gaped vacantly, wracking his brains to try and think of a crushing reply.

'Well, I suppose we'd better make ourselves as comfortable as possible,' sighed Mrs. Bascombe, 'though what I shall look like in the morning when the newspaper people come to take photographs and things, I dread to think. I'm sure I never imagined that blackballing people led to such trouble. Poor, dear George did it once or twice at his club and never got into any bother with the police. I suppose there's been a new act passed, or something.'

'You mean black*mail*,' began Sir Richard, and at that moment the constable burst unceremoniously into the

240

room, his large face full of excitement.

'They've gone, sir!' he announced breathlessly.

'Gone?' Carr's hands clenched involuntarily.

'Both Mr. Silverton's room and the woman's are empty, sir,' the policeman continued quickly. 'There's a communicating door between the two, and the lock's broken.'

Carr's eyes narrowed. 'I was a fool not to think of that,' he muttered. 'How did they get out?'

'The window of Silverton's room is wide open,' panted the man, 'and the sheets and blankets have been twisted into a rope and tied to the bed rail. They can't have been gone long, sir, because I heard movements in the room a few minutes before you sent for me.'

In two strides Carr was at the window. 'Quick!' he snapped over his shoulder as he jerked it open. 'Go up and fetch Mr. Kent and bring him in here. Get everybody in the house in here, and then tell Sergeant Larch and Inspector Wallace to watch the two exits to this room.

They're to let nobody out on any excuse whatever. Hurry, man, and then join me outside!'

He stepped through the window and vanished into the white mist that began to curl sluggishly into the room.

21

Jimmy Weldon

Reginald Stimpson stared after the disappearing figure of the young detective, on his face a ludicrous expression of astonishment. 'I say, things are beginning to move, what!' he exclaimed. 'How priceless! Fancy dear old Silverton being the Shadow after all.'

'You can't be sure that he is,' protested Sonia quickly.

Mr. Stimpson surveyed her with a pitying smile. 'Oh, it's absolutely obvious, old thing,' he said, nodding his head rapidly. 'Otherwise, why should he do the jolly old film stunt from the bedroom window and skedaddle off?'

'I don't think there can be much doubt,' agreed the chief commissioner with conviction, and Mrs. Bascombe shook her head sorrowfully.

'I shall be *most* disappointed if he is,'

she said with a sigh. 'He was *such* a charming man, and a bachelor.'

'I hope he is,' murmured Sonia almost to herself, staring at the empty grate. 'Oh, I hope he is.'

Stimpson looked amazed. 'Good gracious!' he said in astonishment. 'Why do you hope he's a bachelor?'

'I don't mean *that*.' She made an impatient gesture. 'I mean, I hope he's the Shadow.'

The constable re-entered the room hurriedly, accompanied by Willit and Beverley Kent, and marshalling before him a group of frightened servants in various stages of undress who clustered round the door, staring and blinking apprehensively. Without a word the policeman locked the door behind him, crossed to the other door, locked that also, walked over to the window, and went out.

'How are you feeling now, Kent?' asked Sir Richard as the secretary advanced and seated himself on the arm of the settee.

'Much better, thank you, sir,' he replied. 'My head is still a bit sore, but

244

nothing like as much as it was. What's this idea? What have we all been brought down for?'

Sir Richard explained briefly.

'The Silvertons, eh?' said Kent, raising his eyebrows. 'Well, I'm not surprised. I've said all along — '

Suddenly, clear and distinct from outside the house came the sound of two shots fired in quick succession, and they all swung round towards the window.

'I say,' said Mr. Stimpson with a feeble attempt at humour, 'can't you hear the jolly old fog signals plainly?'

No one took any notice of him; they were all staring anxiously towards the oblong parch of fog, which was all that could be seen of the grounds.

'I wonder if Carr's caught them,' muttered Sir Richard; and as if in answer to his words there came another shot, louder and closer, followed by a hoarse cry of pain. The chief commissioner took a step towards the window. 'I'd like to know what's happening out there!' he exclaimed.

'Somebody's shooting, old boy,' answered

Simpson innocently.

'You surprise me!' snapped Sir Richard. He went to the window and was on the point of going out when Sonia stopped him.

'Mr. Carr said none of us was to leave the room,' she reminded him.

He paused on the threshold. 'That doesn't apply to me,' he said sharply and went out, but he did not get far.

Outside on the balcony he ran into a struggling group comprising Carr and Silverton, Moya and the constable. The inspector was gripping the man by the arm and dragging him towards the library window. Clasping his right wrist, and cursing softly below his breath, Silverton was pushed roughly into the room.

'Now then, Silverton, or whatever your name is,' said Carr grimly, keeping the other covered with an automatic, 'let me see what you were digging out from under those bushes.'

Silverton eyed him sullenly, still rubbing his wrist, from which a thin trickle of blood oozed over the back of his hand.

'Come on — quick!' rapped the inspector.

'You've no right to treat us like this!' cried Moya, struggling to free herself from the constable's grasp. 'I appeal to Sir Richard — '

'I'll deal with you later, madam!' snapped Carr. 'At the moment I'm going to see what it is this man took from under those bushes.'

Silverton hesitated, and then with a shrug of his shoulders put his left hand into his pocket, pulled out a flat leather case, and flung it on the floor. 'There you are, damn you!' he snarled viciously. 'I suppose the game is up.'

Without taking his eyes off the man, Carr stooped and, picking up the case, snapped it open. A burst of living fire seemed to spring from the velvet-lined interior, and he lifted out a beautifully graduated diamond necklace.

'So that's it, is it?' he said softly. 'Where did you get this?'

'Find out!' growled Silverton stubbornly.

'Good God!' Sir Richard had advanced

and was staring at the glittering piece of jewellery in amazement. 'Lady Markham's.'

'You recognise it, sir?' asked Carr, turning to him quickly.

The chief commissioner nodded. 'Yes,' he answered. 'It belongs to Lady Markham, of Markham Lodge. She only lives about five miles from here. I've seen it dozens of times.'

Carr looked at Silverton, and his eyes were hard. 'You got the initial letter right when you said you were a broker,' he remarked, 'but you went wrong over the others! Got anything else on you?'

The other compressed his lips and remained silent.

'Lawson, frisk him!' The constable who had been holding Moya by the arm released her and, going over to Silverton, rapidly and expertly ran his hands over the man. From the inside breast pocket of his coat he produced a leather roll, which he handed to his superior.

The young inspector took it, and after a glance at its contents nodded quickly. 'Is that all?' he asked.

'Yes, sir,' answered the constable.

'A complete set of burglar's tools,' said Carr gently. 'I think that's fairly conclusive. Now the question is, who are you?'

Silverton still remained silent.

'Come on, you might as well come clean,' persisted the detective. 'I expect we've got a full account of you in Records.'

The man's lips twisted into a wolfish smile. 'Well, look it up!' he snarled. 'I'm not going to do your job for you!'

'All right,' said Carr evenly. 'But you're not doing yourself any good, my man, by — what's that on your arm?' He broke off suddenly and pointed to a blue tattoo mark that the rucking-up of the man's right sleeve had for a moment revealed on his forearm. Silverton tried to hide it, but the inspector stepped forward and, jerking up the sleeve, studied it closely.

'By jove, I know you now!' he cried. 'You're Jimmy Weldon! There's no mistaking that mark. I've seen it in Records scores of times. No wonder I thought I'd seen you before somewhere. We've been looking for you for a long time — and your wife!' He turned towards the woman, and she snarled round at him like a fury.

'Well, now you've got us, you ought to be satisfied!' she hissed, almost incoherent in her rage. 'We'd have been miles away by now if it hadn't been for the car breaking down and this damned fog.' Her voice broke. 'I knew something like this would happen when I found out where we'd come to!'

'Accidents happen in the best-regulated families,' Carr said lightly. 'I suppose you were working the old trick, eh? Got yourselves invited to a weekend party at Lady Markham's, pinched the necklace at the first opportunity, and cleared out.' He chuckled softly. 'I'll bet this is the first time you've been the guests of a chief commissioner, though! It must have been a nasty shock! You've got another one coming, too. You're wanted for the Big Thing, Weldon. That watchman at Slade & Driver's died — I suppose you know that?' He eyed the other steadily, and the man's face paled.

'It was an accident,' he muttered. 'I never meant to kill him. I only meant to frighten him . . . '

'If you can convince a jury of that,' said Carr, 'you may get off, but I should think it's very doubtful. I suppose you got scared,' he went on, 'when you found that the house was full of police; afraid that the necklace and your kit of burglar's tools might be found. That's what made you sneak out of the passage window and hide them in the bushes, eh?'

Weldon jerked back his head, and there was a hint of defiance in his eyes. 'Look here,' he said calmly, 'if you've got anything further to say, say it and get it done with.' He glared across at the open-mouthed Stimpson, who was watching him, agog with excitement. 'I'm sick of standing here on show for the sake of a lot of goggle-eyed idiots!'

Mr. Stimpson peered at him through his monocle as though he were looking at some strange zoological specimen. 'I say, you know!' he exclaimed. 'You're the first real burglar I've ever seen!'

'Weldon's more than a burglar,' said Carr. 'He's the cleverest safe-breaker in England; and — ' He stopped dead and his eyes suddenly gleamed. 'Weldon,' he almost shouted, 'could you open *that* safe?'

He pointed to the safe in which lay the only piece of evidence against the Shadow.

22

The Shadow

Jimmy Weldon looked at the young inspector in surprise. 'On my head,' he answered. 'But what's the game?'

'There's something in there I want,' said Carr. 'I was going to get a man down from the Yard to open it, but there's no need if you can do it.'

'This is most irregular, Carr,' began the chief commissioner, frowning. 'I don't know that I can — '

'If you say no, sir, of course that's all there is to it,' interrupted the young detective. 'But I should like to point out that if you refuse, you may possibly be destroying our only chance of catching the Shadow.'

Sir Richard hesitated. 'Very well,' he said reluctantly. 'In that case I agree, but I don't like it — it's most unusual.'

'I know it is, sir,' said Carr, 'but it's

necessary. Go on, Weldon.'

'Supposing I do this,' said Weldon, 'what do I get out of it?'

'I can't promise you anything, you know that,' answered the inspector. 'But if the shooting of that watchman was an accident, I'll do what I can to lighten your sentence.'

The man hesitated for the fraction of a second, and then with a jerk of his shoulders went over to the safe. 'All right,' he muttered, 'I'll do it. Give me those tools.'

Carr handed him the leather roll and turned to the constable. 'Unlock the door and let Wallace in,' he ordered; and when the policeman had obeyed, and the burly form of the local inspector entered, he continued: 'Stay by that door, Wallace. Now lock it again, and then unlock the other door and let Larch in.' He looked quickly round the room. 'Larch,' he said as the plainclothes man came in, 'guard that door. You come over here by the window.' He beckoned to the policeman. 'That's all right. Now go ahead, Weldon.'

'What's the idea?' asked Kent curiously.

With his back to the safe, Carr faced them steadily. His jaw was set and the expression on his face was grim. 'The Shadow is in this room,' he answered slowly. 'In a few minutes I hope we shall know who he is.'

The electric atmosphere that had filled the room seemed to discharge in one swift, flashing spark at his quietly spoken words. A sighing breath like wind through a copse of trees escaped from the little group of people watching the tall figure of the youthful inspector.

'I say, this is fearfully thrilling!' drawled Stimpson in what was intended to be a casual tone, but his voice shook with excitement, and his face was eager and intense.

Jimmy Weldon was kneeling before the safe, engrossed in his work; and Carr, as he watched him methodically preparing for the job, knew that it was a labour of love, and that it was for just this reason that the man had reached the top of the tree in his particular line of business.

There was no sound except the faint clink of steel against steel, and the quick irregular breathing of Sonia as she leant forward eagerly, her face white as paper, her slender hands gripping the arms of her chair so tightly that the knuckles showed cream-coloured under the stretched skin.

Five minutes dragged slowly by — five minutes that seemed to those present more like five hours; and then suddenly the man at the safe gave a little low exclamation of triumph. 'Got it!' He only whispered the words, but in that tense silence it sounded as though he had shouted. He rose from his knees, gripped the handle of the safe, and with a jerk of his wrist pulled the door open.

'Stand away from that safe, Weldon,' ordered Carr, and the man obeyed, walking over to the side of his wife and carefully brushing his trousers.

The young inspector stooped and peered into the open safe. After a few minutes' search he took out a small white box. Removing the lid, he lifted out between his thumb and forefinger the tiny gold and platinum trinket that had been found gripped in Elliot's dead hand when his body had been discovered.

'Miss Lane,' he called over to his side, and she came haltingly, while the others instinctively crowded round. 'Have you ever seen this before?' He held the little charm out in the palm of his hand.

She looked at it, turned it over with her finger, and her face went ghastly. 'Yes,' she muttered in a husky whisper.

'What?' Sir Richard pressed forward. 'Sunny, are you — '

'One moment, sir, please!' Carr stopped him with an outstretched arm. 'Now, Miss Lane,' he went on, 'you have seen this somewhere before?' She nodded. 'And you're *sure* it's the same one?'

'Yes.' She moistened her dry lips. 'I remember that scratch across the shiny part of the sphere.' She pointed to a cut across the polished ball that was clasped in the tiny fingers.

'There is no doubt that this belonged to the Shadow.' The inspector spoke slowly and clearly. 'Where did you see it?'

'On — ' began Sonia, but she was interrupted by a quick movement at her side, and the watchful Carr suddenly sprang forward, striking up the pistol that had been aimed at her head.

'No, you don't!' he cried. 'Wallace, Larch, hold him!'

'Damn you!' Helpless in the grip of the two detectives, Reginald Stimpson glared viciously at Carr, his eyes aflame with hatred.

'Good God!' gasped Sir Richard. 'Stimpson? Impossible!'

'It's not impossible, sir,' said Carr, shaking his head grimly. 'It's a fact. There's the Shadow! Miss Lane suspected it directly she heard the description of the charm; she'd seen one like it some months ago on his dressing-table.'

'Why didn't you tell me?' The chief commissioner turned to his frightened daughter, but she remained silent.

'She couldn't be quite certain until she'd seen it,' answered Carr, speaking for her. 'He stole the keys so that the safe couldn't be opened, hoping he could get the charm during the night. As he would have done if he hadn't been surprised by Cosher Jackson.'

'I wish I'd got you on the stairs this evening,' said Stimpson furiously.

'You did your best.' Carr looked at the distorted face calmly. 'You were scared, weren't you, because you thought I suspected something when I told you to go and measure the bathroom. You never had a bath at all; you wetted your face and hair before killing Fleming, and when you rushed across the library and through that door you took off the long coat you were wearing over your pyjamas, waited until everyone was in here, and then pretended to have come down from the bathroom.

'You made your biggest mistake when you tried to throw suspicion on Sir Richard by wiping your pistol on one of his handkerchiefs, saying you'd found it on the landing. I knew you were lying then, because I'd searched every inch of that landing myself previously, and there was nothing there.'

'You're clever, Carr,' panted Stimpson, his face white with rage. 'Cleverer than all the addle-brained idiots they've got at the Yard. They ought to make you chief commissioner for this, instead of that old fool!' He flashed a contemptuous glance at Sir Richard. 'But you'd never have caught me if it hadn't been for Sonia. In spite of all your damned cleverness, I'd have got the better of the lot of you. Brains!' He laughed harshly. 'I've got more brains in my little finger than you'll find in the whole of Scotland Yard!'

'That's enough, Stimpson,' said Carr sternly. 'You'll have an opportunity for making speeches at your trial. Take him away, Wallace.'

For a second Reginald Stimpson stiffened between the men who were holding him, and then with a supreme effort he mastered his rage and walked coolly to the door. On the threshold he turned.

'Well, I suppose I shall have to toddle off,' he remarked pleasantly, reverting to his habitual drawl. 'So long, everybody. I hope it's a case of gone but not forgotten, what?' He paused and looked at Carr steadily. 'You know I told you, old boy, that you'd never catch the bally Shadow without *me*,' he said and, turning, walked quietly out between the two detectives.

23

Last Words

Throughout the sensational trial that followed in due course, Reginald Stimpson remained perfectly cool and calm, surveying the crowded court through his monocle with the same vacuous, inane expression that had deceived so many people into thinking that the brain behind was not particularly intelligent. Only once had anyone seen the real man behind that mask, that glimpse that the people gathered in the library at Green Lanes had caught at the moment of his arrest. Then, for a moment or two, the real calculating, cruel self had broken through the veneer.

He engaged the cleverest of counsels, but all the K.C.'s eloquence — and it was considerable — could do nothing to save him. The judge's summing-up was long, deliberate, and merciless, although at the same time scrupulously fair. And before he was halfway through it, the verdict was a foregone conclusion. Without leaving the box, the jury brought in a verdict of guilty. Stimpson received his sentence without flinching; and neither did he flinch three weeks later when, in the grey dawn of a cold morning, he walked with a firm step from the condemned cell to the death house, and with strapped hands took his place on the trap . . .

★   ★   ★

On the afternoon of the day that saw the passing of the Shadow, two people were strolling in the pale sunlight through St. James' Park. The cold, fresh air had brought a glow to Sonia's checks and a sparkle to her eyes, although at that particular moment her face was grave and thoughtful.

'I can scarcely believe it even now,' she said. 'Reggie always seemed such a harmless sort of person.'

Carr nodded. 'He deceived you, as he deceived everyone else,' he answered.

'When I first saw him I thought he was a rather boring lunatic.'

'It's rather marvellous that he should have been able to keep up that pose,' she said. 'It must have been a terrible strain.'

'I don't think it was a strain at all,' he replied. 'It wasn't all put on; a great deal of it was natural. His stories, for example, were quite genuine. He really did think that he could write thrillers — and he should have been able to do so remarkably well, seeing that he practically lived his plots. And I've got authentic information that he tried his utmost to get them published.'

'Of course, the reason it was so difficult to catch him,' said Sonia after a slight pause, 'was because he knew all the plans that were made before they were put into practice. Father used to discuss most of them with Mr. Kent, and he could easily have overheard.'

'That's undoubtedly what happened,' agreed Carr. 'Well, I'm glad it's all over. Sir Richard looks a new man since the trial; at least ten years younger.'

'That's what Mrs. Bascombe told him

last night,' said Sonia, and there was a twinkle in her eye. 'But it was a great shock for Father; you see, Reggie's father was one of his oldest friends, and he looked upon Reggie almost as if he were his own son.'

'Yes, I know he felt it rather badly at first,' said Carr. 'In fact, it was a long time before he could realise that it wasn't all a dreadful mistake.'

'I shall never forget my feelings when I first heard about the charm,' said Sonia in a low voice. 'It seemed incredible. I'd known Reggie practically since I was a little girl, and it was dreadful to think that he had been responsible for all the horrible things attributed to the Shadow.'

'I think one of the worst things he did,' said Carr, 'was to try and throw suspicion on the man who had been so kind to him. He deliberately went out of his way to try and make us believe that it was Sir Richard we were after.'

'I know,' she answered. 'For a moment, when that handkerchief was found, I wondered if I hadn't made a mistake. I wondered if perhaps the trinket hadn't really belonged to Father; that Reggie had perhaps given it to him. That's why I was so dreadfully uncertain.'

They walked along in silence. Carr had something of importance to say, which did not concern the Shadow, and he was trying desperately to think of a good opening.

'What happened to those two?' asked Sonia suddenly. 'The Weldons?'

Carr, who at that moment was not the least bit interested in the Weldons, and whose thoughts were far away from such mundane matters, jerked them back with difficulty. 'He got fifteen years,' he answered, 'and she got five. He was lucky to escape the death sentence. By the way,' he said, changing the subject abruptly, 'I've been recommended for promotion.'

'Oh, I'm so glad,' she said, and meant it, though the news was not news to her. It was she herself who had suggested the idea to Sir Richard.

He glanced at her out of the corners of his eyes, and his lips parted. But the words that were hovering on the tip of his tongue remained unuttered. For the first time in his life he was feeling unaccountably shy. Hang it, why couldn't he think of a good beginning?

Sonia, who knew exactly what was passing through his mind, and what he was struggling to put into words, was secretly amused. Covertly, she watched his wrinkled brow. She could, perhaps, have made things easier for him had she chosen, but at that moment she didn't choose to. She was rather interested to hear how he would approach the subject without any help from her.

It was a little after four o'clock, and they had the park almost to themselves, which was not surprising; for although the afternoon was fine, it was a little bleak. There was an easterly nip in the wind, and the coming night looked like being a cold one. They walked slowly along the gravel path, side by side, and it was a long time before either of them spoke. It was Carr who eventually broke the silence.

'It seems terribly strange that you and I should be strolling here together,' he said suddenly.

She raised her head from her enveloping furs and looked up at him. 'Why?' she asked.

'Well, doesn't it?' He laughed rather awkwardly. 'A few weeks ago I didn't know you at all, and now ... ' He hesitated. ' ... I feel as if I've known you all my life.'

'I don't think time has got much to do with that,' she said. 'You feel like that about some people.'

'I used to wonder if I'd ever know you better,' he went on, 'when you used to come up to the Yard to see Sir Richard; and I came to the conclusion then that it was very unlikely.'

'Why?' she said again, and smiled. 'Did I look so very formidable?'

'No, but ... ' He was getting a little incoherent. 'Well, I was a very small sound at the Yard, and you were the daughter of the big Noise ... '

She laughed. 'Father would be amused to hear himself described as the big Noise,' she said. 'He's the tiniest murmur imaginable, really. Anyway, you'll be making more noise soon.'

'I shall be a superintendent,' he admitted. 'But there's still a wide gap . . . '

Sonia came to the conclusion that this had gone on long enough. For one thing, she was dying for some tea; and for another, she was getting intensely cold. 'If that's all that's troubling you,' she said calmly, 'I shouldn't worry anymore.'

Something in the tone of her voice made him stop and look at her. In the eyes that were raised to his, he saw an expression that was unmistakable. And to the horror of an elderly lady who was feeding some ducks near the bridge, he took her in his arms and kissed her trembling lips . . .

We do hope that you have enjoyed reading this large print book.

Did you know that all of our titles are available for purchase?

We publish a wide range of high quality large print books including:
Romances, Mysteries, Classics
General Fiction
Non Fiction and Westerns

Special interest titles available in large print are:
The Little Oxford Dictionary
Music Book, Song Book
Hymn Book, Service Book

Also available from us courtesy of Oxford University Press:
Young Readers' Dictionary
(large print edition)
Young Readers' Thesaurus
(large print edition)

For further information or a free brochure, please contact us at:
Ulverscroft Large Print Books Ltd.,
The Green, Bradgate Road, Anstey,
Leicester, LE7 7FU, England.
Tel: (00 44) **0116 236 4325**
Fax: (00 44) **0116 234 0205**

Other titles in the
Linford Mystery Library:

THE GALLOWS IN MY GARDEN

Richard Deming

Grace Lawson and her brother Donald stand to inherit their late father's millions when they reach the age of twenty-one — but someone in their household of family, servants and regular guests seems intent on ensuring they don't live that long. Donald disappears, and a would-be killer dogs Grace's every move. Not wanting to involve the police and create a family scandal, Grace turns to private investigator Manville Moon — who is unaware of how complex the case will be, or that his own life will be threatened . . .

IT'S HER FAULT

Tony Gleeson

An aging university professor insists to Detective Frank Vandegraf that his estranged wife is trying to kill him, but the problem is that she's nowhere to be found. A relative claims that it's the other way around: the husband is actually threatening to kill his wife. When the professor turns up murdered shortly thereafter, with a mysterious note lying on his chest that says 'IT'S HER FAULT', Frank redoubles his efforts to locate the missing wife, his prime suspect. But when he does, the case becomes even more baffling . . .

THE BESSIE BLUE KILLER

Richard A. Lupoff

A film studio sets out to create a documentary about the Tuskegee Airmen, a unit of African-Americans who flew combat missions in World War Two — but filming has barely begun when a corpse is found on the set. Hobart Lindsey, insurance investigator turned detective, enters the scene, aided by Marvia Plum, his policewoman girlfriend. Soon he uncovers a mystery stretching half a century into the past — and suddenly and unexpectedly is flying through a hazardous murder investigation by the seat of his pants!

UNHOLY GROUND

Catriona McCuaig

When midwife Maudie Rouse marries
the love of her life, policeman Dick
Bryant, the pair could not be happier
as they settle into contented domestic-
ity in the village of Llandyfan. But
troubles abound for the newlyweds
— an abandoned baby, a difficult new
district nurse, and the possibility of
losing their home — and Maudie
must find a way to deal with the
problems, in addition to bicycling
around the village performing her
professional duties. Meanwhile, a grim
discovery is made in a local farmer's
field . . .